WE'VE MET BEFORE

MIRIAM O'BOYE

ISBN: 9798301747427

Cover designed using Canva

DEDICATION

For all the girls with a hot boss fantasy.

18+

Playlist

Holiday - Green Day

Money, Power, Fame - Don Broco

ST PATRICK - Pvris

Love In an Elevator - Aerosmith

It's My Birthday - Cody Wise & will.i.am

One For the Road - Arctic Monkeys

Dark Vader - J Hus

Kill Me - Kolby Cooper

Attn. - Beartooth

Life Of the Party - All Time Low

Gungho - Vukovi

What's Wrong - Pvris

Epilogue

Granite - Sleep Token

"In the corporate world, nothing stays secret for long." – Unknown

Trigger/ Content Warnings:

Mentions of a parent with alcoholism (in the past).

Disclaimer:

This is a work of fiction. While this book features a workplace romance, it is entirely made up and not meant to encourage or discourage relationships at work—what you do is up to you! That said, everyone deserves respect and a safe work environment. If you ever experience something in the workplace that makes you uncomfortable or goes against your consent, please speak to someone you trust or seek professional support. Your well-being comes first.

1 MONICA

"Monica! Hurry up before our flight leaves without us!"

Rain screamed from across our university dorm. Rainbow—though she prefers to be called Rain—has been my best friend ever since she transferred to our high school when we were thirteen. Growing up as an only child wasn't always easy, but Rain has always been my rock and continues to be. She stood anxiously at the door, holding our boarding passes and passports, ready to leave cloudy, gloomy Manchester behind.

I walked over to her, calmly stroking her shoulder "Rain, we have three hours until our flight to Italy leaves."

She let out a huff and relaxed her shoulders.

"We've been looking forward to this all summer, I wouldn't miss it for the world"

I assured her and gave her a small smile. With university over and our degrees secured, mine in Marketing and hers in Finance, we could relax and celebrate with a few days in the Italian sun.

We had both been working part time jobs at the pub, The Dog and Gun, my dad owned to save up for our post-graduation trip.

You have earned this, Mon Mon. Reminding myself of what my dad had said to me on the day of my graduation. I gave him the biggest hug that day, as well as Rain's parents, Lee, and Aurora. As much as I love Aurora, I should have been hugging my own mother.

It still hurts to think about it. My mother walked out on me and my father the day before my fourteenth birthday. I remember the weight of it, like something breaking apart inside me, but in truth, she had been gone long before that day. Even when she was around, my father was the one who raised me. My father was the one who moved his entire life from Spain to England to be with my mother. He was the one who made dinner, helped with homework, and showed up for me when it mattered. Meanwhile, she would be off doing fuck knows what with God knows who, or spending nights out at parties, barely a part of our lives. It was as if she was always looking for something else, something we couldn't give her.

When she finally left, it almost destroyed my dad—but a part of me had expected it all along. I have come to terms with her abandonment—we both have—but there's still that lingering part of me that wonders if I'll ever be enough. My mother never deserved him, or me for that matter. I reluctantly sent her an invitation for my graduation, to her last known address. No surprise that she hadn't turned up that day. She would remain forever a disappointment.

Pushing the memory of her holding her bags and walking out the door out of my head, I turned to my best friend who was waiting eagerly by the door, smiling like the Cheshire cat. Waving goodbye to our small but cosy dorm, we locked the door and began our walk down the cold, concrete stairs to the noisy busy streets of Manchester. Rain bounced on the sidewalk like an excited bunny, her long auburn hair flying in the wind and her eyes shining as our Uber pulled up to take us to the airport. We loaded up the boot of the car with our luggage and hopped in.

I leaned back as we drove by looking at the rows of trees on the streets, students heading to graduation parties, families going about their day. I thought about what would be waiting for us upon our return to Manchester: me starting my new role as Marketing Coordinator at a well-established agency and Rain beginning her new job at the local bank. We both also found reasonably sized, and affordable, studio apartments that we would be moving into a week after we landed back in England. Skye, Rain's older sister, and her husband, Steve, own an interior design company and will be helping both of us decorate our new apartments. I grinned, thinking back to Rain and her sister arguing over paint colours a few weeks ago. Their laughter filled the room while they went back and forth about the perfect shade for the walls. It was just a little thing, but it hit me how much we had all grown together.

•·················•·················•

"Cheers" we said in unison, clinking our glasses of prosecco as we sat in one of the airport cocktail bars, waiting for our gate to open. The sounds of children crying, groups of girls and boys laughing, and suitcases being dragged along filled the large terminal. I looked around, feeling a deep sense of satisfaction and happiness. Finishing university was a huge milestone, and now that it was behind me, I felt a weight lift off my shoulders. The anticipation of our holiday was thrilling—an exciting escape from the daily grind. And as I sipped my drink, I couldn't help but feel eager about coming back and starting my new job. It felt like everything was falling into place, and the chaotic buzz of the airport reflected the whirlwind of changes in my life.

Turning to Rain I said to her "so, what are you looking forward to the most on our trip?"

She tapped her lip with her finger, her purple nail polish shining in the light.

"Our trip to the colosseum, all the food we'll eat and hitting some bars to drink some delicious Italian wine."

"No hot summer sex with an Italian man?" I wiggle my eyebrows at her.

"Nope, I will only be making puppy dog eyes for wine and food."

We both burst out laughing. I was so ready to explore the city, relax and drink some wine. We'd both missed out on student nights at local bars and clubs during uni, instead spending our Friday and Saturday nights working at the pub. I looked down at my wrist and ran my fingers over the little airplane tattoo that I had matching with Rain. We had them done when we both turned eighteen. Symbolising our commitment to stay connected, no matter where life takes us.

By the time we knocked back a few glasses of prosecco, our flight information had shown up on the screen. Feeling slightly buzzed as I stood up, we made our way, through the busy crowds of holiday makers and solo travellers, towards our designated gate. After swiftly making our way through security, we boarded the plane and finally sat down in our seats. I fastened my belt and let out a deep exhale as we listened to the pilot's announcement.

"Welcome aboard our ten-thirty flight to Rome, Italy, the flight time is two and a half hours. We hope you enjoy the journey." Rain turned to face me with the biggest smile on her face.

"Mon, I am so excited! We have waited so long for this. I cannot believe we are spending your twenty fourth birthday in Italy!" Rain's eyes sparkled as she leaned over and placed a kiss on my cheek.

"I have a feeling this is going to be the best birthday yet!" she nodded her head in agreement and sank into her seat.

My phone buzzed in my hand. I turned the screen toward Rain, showing her a message from my dad. She pushed her curls behind her ears as I tied up my thick black hair into a messy bun.

Padre:

Have a safe flight!

Me:

Thanks Dad!

Padre:

Look after Rain!

Me:

Will do! Love you!

'How is Carlos?' she asked, glancing up after reading it.

"He's good. He is thinking of asking the woman who owns the cafe opposite the pub, out on a date." Responding to her shocked face, I held my hands up in the air.

"I'm just as shocked as you." My mother's lawyer had reached out to my father, notifying him of their divorce, a few years after she left. He has been focused on the pub ever since. He deserves to be with someone who is going to appreciate and love him.

I pushed up the hood of my jumper and put in my earphones, trying to contain my own bubbling excitement. I shimmied down in my seat, closed my eyes and let my mind wander—drifting through thoughts of where my life was heading.

2 CHASE

"I need a fucking break" I mumbled to myself as I walked through the doors of the meeting room. I took a seat at the top of the table and glanced around the room, eyes on my team as I waited for their updates.

"Revenue is up almost twenty-five percent this quarter, Mr. Marino" Jane, one of my junior associates, spits out from across the table. She has been trying to get into my pants since the Christmas party last year, where we engaged in a very drunken kiss. That was a huge mistake, I try not to sleep with women I work with. It gets messy, I don't do messy. I do casual or one-night stands.

Trying to not sound too frustrated, I told the team, "We can do better. I expect everyone to put in their best effort." I emailed Jane before our meeting reminding her that she will be training our new hire when they begin in a few weeks. The team responded with a round of nods.

I push them hard because that is exactly what my parents did when I told them I was starting my own business. When I started 'Be Creative' ten years ago, just shy of my twentieth birthday, I wanted it to be the best marketing agency in Manchester. In the last decade we have won awards, taken on board huge clients, and opened offices in London, the U.S. and as of next year Australia. You can always do better. Do more. I want more. I am always searching for more. My parents seem to think settling down, finding a wife, and starting a family will be that more I'm looking for. I beg to differ. At least my brother Jordan agrees with me. We had made a deal that he would only settle down when I did. It's not like I haven't had girlfriends in the past.

I was constantly told that I cared about the business more than them. Sure, I might have missed a date or two here and there, which eventually contributed to those relationships fizzling out. But there is nothing quite so thrilling as striking a hard-won deal, which meant late nights and working away. Which is why casual and one night stands work better for me.

The meeting went on for another forty-five minutes, discussing contracts, negotiations, and internal business updates. Feeling slightly constricted within these four walls, I let out a sigh, the weight of the room's atmosphere pressing on me.

"I will be taking some time off and will be returning

in a few days. We will regroup then. Meeting dismissed."

The words felt like a release, a small but significant step towards reclaiming my sense of freedom and space. The routine and pressures of the past weeks had taken their toll, and the idea of stepping away, even for just a short while, was tempting. As my team shuffled out of the room, I pulled out my phone and called Jordan, running my fingers through my hair.

"Chase, to what do I owe the pleasure?" Jordan chirped down the phone, he was in a good mood. "Book a flight. Anywhere. I need some time away from this place" I could hear him tapping on his keyboard.

"So, there's a flight to New York leaving tomorrow morning." He replied a few minutes later. I contemplated it but I needed something sooner.

"Or there's a flight to Rome leaving in a few hours."

Italy it is. "Book two seats to Rome" I let out a strained huff.

"You are coming with me brother. Let us kick back for a few days." I could practically hear the cogs turning in his head.

"Fuck it, why not. We should celebrate the opening of my new dealership." *Show off.*

"Right. Text me with the details. I'll meet you outside my apartment in a few hours."

I ended the call and walked down the corridor of the building. I pressed the call button for the elevator and rode it down to the main lobby and out to the car park. Sliding into the driver's seat of my grey BMW M5—a birthday gift from Jordan—I took a moment to appreciate the luxury and power of the car before heading to my apartment.

Jordan, who is two years older, had accomplished so much already. Around the same time I launched Be Creative, he opened his first high-end dealership, Elite Cars. Now, just a few weeks away from the grand opening of his tenth location, his success was as impressive as ever. I walked through the front door of my apartment, threw my suit jacket and briefcase onto the sofa with a satisfying thud, letting the weight of the day slip from my shoulders. My gym bag followed, collapsing in a heap beside them. Without hesitation, I headed to the kitchen, my mind already fixed on one thing. I grabbed a glass and poured myself a double shot of whiskey. I took a long, slow sip, letting the warmth spread through me as I leaned against the cool marble counter and I glanced around, appreciating the quiet hum of the apartment. The red leather sofas gleamed under the custom lighting, their bold colour contrasting beautifully against the polished wood floors. I loved every detail, from the sleek lines of the furniture to the marble counters. My interior designer did an amazing job, as she did with a few other apartments that I owned. My eyes lingered on the dozens of awards lined up on the shelves—a tangible reminder of the years of relentless effort. I took another sip, the whiskey burning pleasantly down my throat, and I felt a swell of pride. This was mine—every inch of it—and in that moment, I allowed myself to feel the full weight of everything I had built.

So why did it feel like I constantly wanted more? Shaking my head, I left the kitchen and headed to the bathroom for a quick shower. After getting dressed, I threw a few t-shirts, shorts, and shoes into a small suitcase. My phone vibrated with a text from Jordan.

Jordan (Dickhead):

Your carriage awaits, princess.

Me:

On my way down fuck face

I exhaled as I locked the door behind me, thinking about how much I needed this last-minute trip to unwind and clear my head. Jordan had hired a driver, a sleek limousine, and by the time I slid into the plush interior, he had already popped open a bottle of champagne. His flamboyant display was so typical of him—part of me rolled my eyes, but another part could not help but smile. It was nice to catch up with Jordan; our lives had become so hectic that these moments were rare. As we eased into the champagne and let the bubbles tickle our senses, we swapped updates on family gossip and business dramas. Jordan's grin grew wider as he brought up a topic that made me want to groan.

"So, mother was asking about your dating life," he said, his eyes twinkling mischievously. I felt a flash of irritation.

"What did you tell her?" I shot back, already bracing for his response.

"I didn't tell her much," Jordan said, barely containing his laughter. "Just that you're busy running the company and that you enjoy picking up one-night stands in bars". My immediate reaction was to grab a handful of ice from the bucket and hurl it at him, but he just chuckled, brushing the ice off with a shrug.

"I'm joking. Lighten up."

As he picked ice from his jacket, the limo came to a stop. We gathered our bags, tipped the driver, and headed inside the departure hall.

•················•·················•

We entered the airport, and I checked my watch, pleased to see that I had time for a quick shot of whiskey. Ushering us over to a bar, I ordered two shots. We cheered and downed our shots. Enjoying that warm feeling falling down the back of my throat. Jordan and I knocked back a few more before paying our tab and walking out. We made our way through security and stood in the queue waiting to have our boarding passes and passports checked. He gave me a smirk and a rude gesture. I punched him in his shoulder. It was easy to do as Jordan and I were the same height both standing tall at six foot three, but where his hair is dark blonde in colour, mine is chestnut brown. We both have deep brown eyes and dark olive skin, traits inherited from our parents, who originate from Northern Italy. Despite my mother being slightly interfering at times, I have always been so grateful for our parents. Our mother and father had retired last year and moved back to Verona. Back to the town where my ancestors lived.

"Let's keep the line moving people." the flight attendant told us and the queue of people behind us. "Let's get this party started" sang Jordan. I rolled my eyes. I might just regret this trip. I hope that something more rears its beautiful head.

3 MONICA

The heat of the sun slapped me in the face as soon as the plane doors opened. Embracing the warm feeling, I reached into my backpack and grabbed my sunglasses. We were ushered down the steps of the plane and began our walk over to 'Arrivals.' Holding my pinky finger and swinging my hand, Rain let out a small giggle. We walked inside and towards baggage claim.

"I think those are our bags over there."

"Rain, who else has a pink suitcase with dreamcatchers on?"

Grunting as we grabbed our bags, we walked outside to call for a taxi to take us to our hotel. I took a second to appreciate that heat from the sun warming my skin. Our hotel was located right near the Trevi

Fountain and a short distance from the colosseum. During our ride to the hotel, I looked around at the scenery of Rome. So many cosy cafes and gorgeous restaurants. The smell of pizza, leaving me feeling slightly hungry and the aroma of hot coffee filling the summer air. We pulled up to our hotel, grabbed our bags and walked inside. We were given our key cards and headed up to our rooms. Naturally, Rain's room was next to mine. She smiled as we both walked inside our rooms and closed the door behind us.

I walked into my room and instantly felt relaxed. White soft sheets on the bed, fresh flowers on the vanity, the tops of the beautiful green trees that I could see from my hotel window. I started unpacking and hanging up my clothes and evening dresses, in the wardrobe. I tied up my hair and removed my clothes, determined to take a shower as quickly as possible. The shower had amazing pressure and steam. After a few minutes under the hot water, I washed and turned off the water. Stepping out of the bathroom, I caught my reflection in the standing mirror. I adored my new haircut; I usually wore my hair long but decided for new beginnings I would try a new style. So, my hair went from almost touching the bottom of my spine to chest level. From the wardrobe, I pulled out a black slim cocktail dress that would smooth over my curves, along with some silver strappy heels. After dressing, I applied red lipstick, grabbed my purse, and knocked on Rain's door.

"Hey, ready to get some food?" I asked her when she opened the door. Rain opted for a red dress that pushed up her breasts and some very classy black chunky heels

"Hell yeah, let's get some pizza ASAP." She squealed.

"You look amazing by the way; you have to let me borrow that dress."

She bent at the knees and gave me a small courtesy that made me chuckle.

We pushed the call button for the lift and rode down to reception and walked onto the streets of Rome. It was only a short walk to a gorgeous bar and restaurant that was highly recommended on the internet. The waiter brought us over to the bar and told us our table would be ready in a few minutes. "Two red wines please. Make them large" I told the bartender. With a nod, he started pouring. I let out a deep exhale. The sounds of couples dining, waiters taking orders and the smells of food from the kitchen filled the restaurant.

"Let the birthday celebrations begin" Rain exclaimed with joy.

"It's your birthday?" the bartender who served us our drinks asked me in his alluring Italian accent. "Technically, it's tomorrow but yes we're celebrating my birthday and our graduation" I said as I pointed my wine glass in Rain's direction. He began pouring out vodka into tall shot glasses.

"Enjoy" he said as he placed them in front of us. We giggled as we downed the shots.

One of the waiters approached us, "Ladies, your table is ready."

After eating our weight in pizza and ice cream, we walked out of the restaurant and admired the sky as the sun started to set. We walked down the street and spotted a bar. We walked inside and sat down at the booth style tables. "I'll grab us some drinks from the bar, wait here" I said to Rain. She gave a small nod. I walked over to the already crowded bar and asked the bartender for two glasses of white wine. A few minutes later, the bartender returned with our drinks. As the night went on, we took turns grabbing the drinks from the bar. We laughed, drank, and enjoyed our first night away from home.

"Just going to freshen up" I told Rain as I stood up from the table to walk over to the bathrooms. I stumbled in, washed my hands, and looked into the mirror to reapply my lipstick. Determined not to lose this lipstick, as I had with so many others I had bought in the past, I tried to slip it back into my clutch as I pushed open the door to exit the bathroom, trying not to stumble over, and failing. I bumped into a tall man walking through the corridor.

"I am so sorry. I might have had one too many wines" I blurted out, feeling my face go warm with slight embarrassment. He stared at me, and I looked at him up and down, focusing on his dark hair, his light bronze skin and deep brown, almost black, eyes. He gave me a coy smirk and slowly brought his hand up to my face to wipe something from my cheek.

"Lipstick" it felt as if his voice vibrated against the walls of where we were standing. He chuckled and walked into the men's bathroom. *Definitely one too many glasses of wine*. Still in slight awe, I walked back over to our table where Rain was sitting.

"Everything okay?"

"You looked flushed" she asked, her eyebrows furrowing.

"Everything is great." I sank into my seat and took a sip of wine.

I took a second to collect my thoughts (and fucking hormones.)

"Wanna dance?"

There she was again with that Chesire cat smile.

"Yes please," we jumped up and I grabbed her hand to lead us to the dance floor. The DJ played song after song, as Rain and I danced until our feet went numb. Lost in the feeling of the bass and the music bouncing from the speakers, I had completely lost track of time. My eyes almost popped out of my head. It was three am.

"Rain, we need to go" I shouted, doubting she even heard me over the loud music. She did. She turned towards me, giggled, and looped her arm through mine. We walked out of the bar and down the street to our hotel. My bed was calling me, and my feet were ready to part ways with these heels. "Hey, it's officially your birthday Mon" Rain said with a slight slur.

"It sure is,"

She proceeded to sing happy birthday the loudest she could, all the way back to the hotel.

The loud buzz of my phone alarm jolted me awake. Groaning, I fumbled for it on the bedside table to silence the noise. It felt as though I had only just closed my eyes. With a sigh, I swung my legs over the edge of the bed, the cold floor sending a shiver up my spine.

A wince escaped my lips as the familiar ache in my feet returned, a lingering reminder of last night, or this morning rather. I walked over to the bathroom, turned on the cold tap and splashed freezing water on my face and brushed my teeth. After a hot shower, I got dressed, slipped on some denim shorts, a grey tank top and white trainers as my outfit of choice for our trip today. Gathering my hair into a high ponytail with one hand, I closed the door to my room with the other before heading over to knock on Rain's door.

"Morning birthday girl," she squealed, grabbing my arms.

"Morning Rain, thank you. How did you sleep? I feel like my head is too heavy to hold up"

I complained. She smiled and handed me a bottle of water with two pain killers from her bag. Life saver. After swallowing a huge gulp of water to wash the pain killers down with, Rain closed the door to her room, and we skipped down the corridor to the lift. We entered the breakfast room, where the aroma of freshly brewed coffee filled the air. A spread of warm cream pastries, ripe, juicy fruit, and a couple of celebratory birthday mimosas awaited us. I really needed this food.

With our hangovers worn off slowly and our energy

restored from breakfast, we stepped out of the hotel and began our leisurely walk toward the Great Colosseum of Rome.

The excitement of the day ahead buzzed in the air as we made a few stops at charming gift shops along the way, each one filled with trinkets and keepsakes. I smiled, remembering to pick up a magnet for my dad. He loves these things. We snapped videos, posed for a photo with the soldiers that were reenacting ancient Rome and climbed what felt like an endless number of steps. The irresistible aroma of pizza and pasta drew us toward a cosy restaurant nestled beside the Colosseum. We ate in comfortable silence, savouring every bite of the hot, cheesy pasta and pepperoni pizza we had decided to share. Each taste seemed to melt away the world around us, as if, in that moment, nothing else mattered.

After a few hours of exploring, we were ready to head back to the hotel. During the ride up to our rooms, Rain turned to me with a playful smile.

"Hey, how about we go back to that bar tonight to celebrate your birthday?"

"Sounds perfect."

The memory of the stranger touching my cheek pops into my head. I wonder if he will be there tonight. After freshening up, we changed into our evening outfits. I slipped into my favourite silver, sparkly dress with a deep V cut that was reserved for special nights out, its shimmer making me feel a little more radiant, a little more special.

Once dressed, I made my way to Rain's room,

excitement bubbling beneath the surface. As I entered, I caught a glimpse of myself in her mirror, taking a moment to admire the way the dress hugged my curves perfectly and made my tits look great, its glitter catching the light. Where some girls were slimmer, I had a little extra, especially on my thighs.

I smiled, feeling both nervous and exhilarated. Rain was still getting ready, carefully curling her hair while applying her makeup with the kind of precision she always had.

I sat down on her bed, the air between us warm with the shared anticipation of the night ahead. Rain finished getting ready and walked over to the corner of the room to pull something out of her bag.

Of course, Rain had brought with her a pink sash that said Happy Birthday in silver glitter, for me to wear. She reached up, threw the sash over me, and pinned the sash to the shoulder of my dress and placed a small kiss on my cheek. We snapped a few selfies for Instagram, and I sent one to my dad.

Padre:

Have a great night, muñeca

Me:

Thanks Dad! Te amo!

My dad has called me a 'doll' since I was a kid. He said it reminds him of how small and cute I was as a baby. Digging around in my bag, I searched for my red lipstick. I rolled my eyes. I had lost another one. I really needed to start bulk buying lipsticks.

4 CHASE

We landed in Rome early in the afternoon and made our way to our hotel from the airport in yet another limousine that Jordan had hired. His obsession with limousines was fascinating. We entered the penthouse suite that we would be staying in for the duration of our trip and sat down to enjoy the view of the city.

"Drink?" Jordan asked, looking out from the window.

"Double" I responded.

He walked to the mini bar and poured the golden liquid into two glasses, which was more than a double shot. He chuckled as he handed me one of the glasses.

"I need to make a few calls and answer a couple of emails before we head out" he sat down on the leather sofa and pulled out his laptop. I rolled my eyes; we were meant to be celebrating.

"Sure, but I'm not waiting for you all night."

He just waved his hand at me. Feeling annoyed but proud of my brother at the same time. I chugged the rest of my drink, stood up, and headed to one of the master bedrooms. I peeked inside and saw a king-sized bed with silky red sheets, a huge window that reached the floor, and a door leading to a fancy bathroom. The room was gorgeous.

"This one is mine" I called out to Jordan.

"All yours" was all he responded with.

I glanced down at my watch, realising the time, I dialled down to reception and ordered some room service for dinner. After unpacking my clothes and grabbing a shower, there was a knock at the door. The waiter pushed the trolley inside and began unloading plates of salad, pizza, fries as well as traditional cakes and pastries onto the kitchen island. I pushed a small wad of cash into his shirt pocket. Grazie. He gave me a small nod and walked out. Jordan wandered over to the island and started stuffing fries into his mouth.

"I'm going to eat and head to the bar downstairs," I said.

He nodded, his mouth full as he mumbled, "Let me finish this email and I'll meet you down there. Order me a drink."

He piled more food onto his plate and went back to his laptop. I walked over and entered my room to get dressed. I pulled on a pair of black shorts and ironed a crisp white shirt, trying to shake off the restlessness that had been gnawing at me. With a quick spray of aftershave, I grab my keycard, take a deep breath, and walk out the door. I hit the call button for the lift and stepped in when it reached my floor. I strolled out into the reception area a few minutes later, it was a small, grounding moment amid everything.

The bar was conveniently located right inside the hotel lobby, a welcome sight after a day that felt too long. I pushed through the doors and made my way to a quiet table tucked into a cosy corner, hoping to find a bit of peace amidst the buzz. The bar's interior struck a charming balance between elegance and modernity. It had a sleek, rounded bar that gleamed under soft lighting. The black-and-white checkered dance floor added a touch of retro flair. The DJ and speakers set off to one side. The atmosphere was inviting, a blend of sophistication and laid-back vibes, perfect for unwinding and finding a moment of solace.

I sat down at the table and a waiter came over to take my order. I was almost four whiskey glasses deep and there was still no sign of Jordan. I checked my phone and noticed he hadn't responded to any of the messages I'd left him. I bet he's fallen asleep. The bar was booming with people, but I was starting to feel restless again. Downing Jordan's glass that had been waiting for him, I stood up from the table and walked down the corridor to the bathroom. As I made my way down the hall, someone burst out of the women's bathroom and collided with my chest. She looked up at me with wide eyes, her cheeks flushing a deep red.

"I'm so sorry," she stammered, a hint of

embarrassment in her voice. "I might've had one too many wines."

The breath caught in my chest as I stared at her. Her hair, dark as midnight, framed a face so smooth it seemed to glow in the soft, dim light. Her deep, chocolate-brown eyes held me captive, pulling me in with an intensity I'd never felt before. I am not sure I'd stared into a woman's eyes before. She flicked her hair behind her shoulder, the smell of cherries hit me. I noticed she had something on her cheekbone. I slowly brought my hand up to her face and pushed down lightly to remove the same red lipstick that she had painted on her lips.

"Lipstick"

I whispered to her. I chuckled and walked inside the men's bathroom. After washing my hands, I headed back down the corridor and spotted a small black container lying near the ladies' bathroom door. Curious, I crouched down, picked it up, and flipped it open. Red lipstick. Without a second thought, I slipped it into the pocket of my shorts and continued on my way.

The bar was buzzing with energy as I wove through the crowd and took the lift to the top floor. Entering the peace and quiet of my suite, I wasn't surprised to find Jordan sprawled out on the sofa, fast asleep. A groan escaped me as I switched off his laptop and hauled him to one of the master bedrooms. He mumbled incoherently as I dropped him onto the bed.

Shutting his door, I retreated to my own room. My shirt and shorts were off in moments, folded neatly onto the vanity table.

As I stood brushing my teeth, I walked over to my shorts, reached into the pocket, and pulled out the lipstick. Turning it over in my hand, I walked to the bedside table and set it down. Maybe tomorrow, I'd have the chance of returning it to her.

5 CHASE

The next morning, I got dressed into my gym clothes and closed the door to my room. I knocked on Jordan's door and shouted to him that I would be heading down to use the gym.

"Wait. Give me five minutes to get dressed and I'll come with you" he shouted back.

"Fine but hurry up Jordan."

I walked over to the kitchen island, where the coffee machine was, and pushed the espresso button. I repeated this a second time, for Jordan's espresso. He shuffled out of his room and over to the island. He brought his coffee to his mouth and tipped his cup up at me.

"Anything eventful happen last night?" he said as he nudged my shoulder. God, he is as bad as our mother.

"Nope," I lied. "Come on, I want to get a good workout before we go out today."

We rode the lift to the hotel basement and opened the gym doors. We started on weights, then machines and finished with a few laps around the indoor pool. My muscles instantly relax as soon as I sat down in the sauna.

"What do you want to do today?"
Jordan asked, with beads of sweat dripping down his forehead.

"Let's hit a few of the clothing shops, try a few gelato shops. Dinner and drinks in the hotel bar." His gaze shifted towards me; his expression filled with confusion.

"What?" I snapped.

"It's not very often you have a drink in the same place, let alone two nights in a row" he said.

I shrugged and tipped my head back and told him, "It's a good bar, that's all."

We weren't short of bars and restaurants in Rome. But I wanted to see if that girl was there again.

We headed to the locker rooms and got dressed back into our clothes. After returning to our suite, we each took a quick shower and slipped into fresh evening clothes. Jordan went with a black shirt and trousers, while I chose a white shirt paired with navy trousers. We headed out to Via dei Condotti, a street known for its designer stores in Rome. We grabbed a few new shirts from Versace, and we made our way to a gelato store. Coffee was usually my choice of flavour but today I had a craving for the flavour cherry. Suddenly I became aware of my new love for the colour red.

"Ready to head back and hit the hotel bar?" Jordan asked me, as we walked out of the gelato store.

"Sure, brother. There is a bottle with our name on it."

Once we returned to the hotel, I sent Jordan upstairs to place our bags in the suite and I went to find us a table inside the bar. It was already quite busy for a Saturday night, but I quickly spotted a free booth in the corner of the room. Cutting my way through the crowd of people over to the booth, I signalled to the bartender to bring over a bottle of whiskey and two glasses. Jordan sat down across from me, just as the waiter placed the bottle on the table. He pulled out a deck of cards from his trouser pocket. I nodded. After a few rounds of drinks and cards, I stood up and made my way up to the bar to order another bottle. I leaned against the bar waiting to be served and took a second to appreciate my surroundings. This break has given me a small window to think about how things are going with the company. My chaotic world is becoming less chaotic, and I need something that will give me the same thrill I had when I started the company. My bank account has grown to a comfortable size, even after investing in other ventures. The constant string of one-night stands is becoming less and less challenging.

I swear I was only gone for a couple minutes. But when I walked back to the table, I saw two girls sitting with Jordan. One with fiery curly auburn hair, the other with sleek, raven black. Just as I started to get closer, the girl with black hair glanced my way and quickly turned her head, trying to hide a laugh.

It *was* her.

6 MONICA

We took the lift down to the reception and stepped outside the hotel, ready to begin our night. As we made our way down the lively street, a few strangers called out "Happy Birthday!" with cheerful smiles. The energy of a bustling Saturday night surrounded us as we headed toward the bar, the city alive with excitement. Making our way immediately to the bar, we each ordered a limoncello cocktail, a classic Italian drink. Enjoying the refreshing burst of lemon from my drink, I glanced around the bar and realised finding a table might be challenging. But instead of worrying about it, I decided to embrace the energy and music from the bar. We danced to the thumping beats of the DJ, cocktails in hand and clutch bags swaying, letting myself get lost in the lively atmosphere.

Feeling lost in the music I almost didn't feel someone tapping my shoulder. I wondered if it was him. I turned around to face a man with blonde hair, dressed in a sleek black shirt and matching trousers. His eyes held a confidence as he spoke, "Hey, I was watching you and your friend dance."

Rain and I couldn't help but laugh, knowing full well our dance moves were far from sexy.

"I was wondering," he continued, a playful smile tugging at the corner of his lips, "if you'd like to join me and my brother for a drink?"

Rain and I exchanged a silent nod, both content to join him. He guided us to a rounded cosy booth tucked in the corner of the bar, its deep red leather seats promising comfort. We slid across the cool leather, settling on the right side. He eased into the seat across from us. His hand gestured towards the bar.

"My brother is just grabbing us another bottle."

He smiled in our direction, focusing his eyes on Rain. Good for her. Whilst I had casual boyfriends and the odd hook up during uni, Rain only had eyes for her degree.

"My name is Jordan. What are your beautiful ladies' names?" Jordan questioned us. From the corner of my eye, I could see Rain blushing.

"This is Monica and my name is Rain."

Jordan let out a huge laugh "Let me guess, your sister is called Cloud."

I quickly turned my head to the side, biting my lip as I brought a hand to my mouth, trying to stifle the laugh bubbling up inside me.

"Her name is Skye actually."

Jordan smacked the table, and we all burst out laughing. Rain nudged my arm bringing my attention to Jordan as he wiped a tear from his eye. I had a feeling this was going to be a very memorable birthday.

"Ah, there he is," Jordan said, as a tall man with dark hair and the same piercing brown eyes as Jordan took a seat across from me.

"This is Chase."

God. He's as sexy as I remember him being. Last night in the dark I couldn't appreciate the his facial features, but in the dimmed light of the bar I can see everything perfectly. My heart felt like everyone around could hear it thudding. He was insanely good looking, and he knew it. My eyes were drawn to his arms, covered in tattoos, each one tracing along his huge muscles. I wonder if those tattoos went all the way across his chest. His fingers felt rough against my soft skin as he extended his hand across the table to shake my hand. I introduced myself and Rain to him.

"It's very nice to meet you both."

Feeling slightly nervous, I shuffled in my seat and corrected my birthday sash that had seemed to have moved whilst I was dancing. Chase tipped his glass in my direction.

"Happy Birthday."

I thanked Chase and felt my face blush.

Was I blushing over a man saying happy birthday? *Pull yourself together Monica.* Chase left the table for a moment to run up to the bar to grab two extra glasses. When he returned, he poured two fingers worth of whiskey into each glass. He pushed one of the glasses in my direction and the other towards Rain. I took a sip, and my throat immediately warmed. Jordan had a crude sense of humour, causing Chase to roll his eyes every time he told a joke. My ribs began to hurt from how much I was laughing. At some point we all switched to drinking water, clearly all enjoying the night and the company without wanting to get drunk.

After a while Jordan and Rain began their own conversation. I lifted my head and glanced across the table; Chase patted the area next to him suggesting that I join him. I stood and quickly moved next to him. I tried not to laugh as he elbowed Jordan in the ribs, telling him to move further down the booth. As I sat down next to Chase, the warm scent of sandalwood and citrus filled my lungs. He turned toward me, his eyes gleamed under the lights of the bar. I noticed a small smirk playing on his lips.

"Any birthday wishes?" he asked, his deep voice rumbling like distant thunder, tinged with a hint of amusement. I'm glad I sobered up, or else I would've asked for a body shot. I'm sure he had the body to match the muscles on his arms. I shook my head instead, not trusting myself to speak.

Chase leaned over, slowly tucked my hair behind my ear and whispered.

"I actually have a gift for you,."

A shiver of goosebumps rippled across my skin, and my palms turned clammy. I discreetly wiped them against the cool fabric of my dress, praying he wouldn't notice.

"It's upstairs in my hotel room".

My spine stiffened. I looked over and I didn't want to interrupt Rain while she was deep in conversation with Jordan, so I pulled my phone out of my bag and left the bag on the table. It was my way of showing her I'd be back and wasn't just disappearing all night. We both stood up from the table and Chase held out his hand. Our fingers laced together perfectly as I allowed him to lead the way.

We made our way to the back of the bar where there was a resident only entrance, he swiped his keycard and opened the door.

Please don't be a serial killer.

My heels clicked against the marble floor in the reception. Slowing my steps I took a second to take in how gorgeous this hotel is. The soft sound of water trickling from the little fountain in the centre is so calming. The reception area is bright and open, with cosy seating and this huge, sparkling chandelier that makes everything feel a bit fancy, but not too over the top. I can't help but wonder how much it must cost to stay somewhere like this—I bet it's not cheap. I let out a deep exhale as Chase pushed the call button for the lift. He reached over, fingers brushing my skin as he tucked my hair behind my shoulder. I was cautious of how busy the hotel reception was, but the world seemed to slow as he leaned in, his lips finding the curve of my neck. A deep groan escaped from his throat.

"You smell so good."

His voice, low and intoxicating, had a way of melting me every time he spoke, flooding me with warmth that made my pulse race.

The lift doors slid open, and Chase's hand gently guided me inside, his fingers pressed firmly against my lower back. I spun on my heels, my back pressed against the cool glass mirror, sending a shiver down my spine. His palms found the surface behind me, caging me in, the warmth of his presence igniting the air between us. The smell of his aftershave filled the space around us. God, he smelt delicious.

He lowered his head, tracing soft kisses along my jawline before descending to my collarbone. I lifted my hands, threading my fingers through his silky hair, pulling him closer as a thrill raced through me. He brought one hand down from the mirror and began pulling up my dress, stopping just as the doors opened to the floor of the penthouse suite.

I *fucking* hate lifts. I was glad my new apartment didn't have one.

Chase grabbed my hand and pulled me as he scanned his keycard to his room. Once we were inside, I looked around in amazement. The suite had a classy but modern vibe to it, the pristine white leather sofas, the kitchen island with coffee maker, the glass coffee table all complementing each other. Chase closed the door behind him and gestured towards the bedroom. I walked over, my legs feeling a little weak. The room was infused with the rich scent of sandalwood and a hint of citrus which must have been the lingering trace of his aftershave. Chase slipped into the room and stood himself in front of me.

Towering over me, he came close and whispered, "close your eyes."

I felt like a kid again, just like on my tenth birthday, waiting for presents. It was rare for my mum to be home for my birthday. I had spent the day with my grandparents, then walked in to find all my friends and family crammed into the kitchen, waiting for me. My mum, stumbling like Bambi, came over and told me to close my eyes. (Not long after that, things turned to shit.)

I shook my head and chuckled, shaking off the memory and focusing on what was happening right now. I placed my phone onto the bed and did as I was told.

"You can open them now."

I opened my eyes to find Chase holding a small black container in front of me. I almost jumped to grab the lipstick. My red lipstick.

"Where did you find this?"

My voice sounded a little too ecstatic to be happy over a lipstick.

"I found it after you stumbled into me last night. Thought it might be important, so I kept a hold of it."

That sent small butterflies down to my stomach. How can this guy be so hot and so sweet?

"Thank you so mu-," Chase closed the distance before I could finish my sentence.

His lips came crashing down on mine. Letting out a small whimper, I gave into his lips, his tongue, his hands all over my dress. The sounds from car horns outside, music from the streets, people in the hotel corridor talking all became quiet and distant. His mouth was hot against mine and I could still taste hints of whiskey in his mouth. He ran his hands up and down my arms, causing small electric shocks to shoot up and down my skin. The kiss was hot and desperate. Chase's lips were soft against my lips, and he tugged at my lower lip as I moaned.

Our feet shifted together until the back of my legs hit the edge of his bed frame. He slid his arm under my lower back and slowly lowered us. The silk sheets instantly cooled my skin. I could feel Chase's heartbeat against my chest. His lips felt soft against my collarbones, where he planted small kisses and began slowly moving down my body. I could feel his hard length digging into my stomach, which made my core begin to throb.

He dropped to his knees at the edge of the bed and pushed my legs open. Chase raised his head and locked eyes with mine.

"Is this okay?"

"Yes," I answered, trying to catch my breath.

This is not something I would normally do but, if I was spending my birthday in Rome with a hot stranger, it would be rude not too. But I suppose that's the small beauty of one-night stands, you'll never see them again.

His hands grazing my inner thigh caused my core throb even more as he tugged at the sides of my thong, pulling them down to my heels. I threw my head back as he dove straight for my clit with his tongue. Chase let out a deep groan. My hands tangled in his hair again. He began giving quick but firm strokes with his tongue to my pussy, slowly pushing two fingers inside me. His moaning was enough to make me come. Which I felt was very quickly approaching, which usually didn't happen so soon. Or at all sometimes.

"Breath for me, Cherry" Chase peered up and ordered me.

"Okay." I breathed in.

I exhaled just as I was hitting that high and felt my entire body vibrate. My eyes rolled back, and I slapped a hand over my mouth, unsure if I was trying to stop myself from screaming or asking Chase to call me that name again. I threw my arm over my head and tried to catch my breath again. Chase ducked into the bathroom to grab a washcloth and returned to clean the release that was now running down my thighs. He gently pulled my underwear back up, my silver sequined dress back down and lifted me from the bed back to my feet.

I leaned into him, "that was…" I began to say.

His eyes darkened as he took a step forward, "Happy birthday, Cherry."

That cute little nickname was starting to do things to me.

7 CHASE

Monica and I stepped into the lift, descending back to the bar. A soft giggle escaped her lips as I playfully cupped her ass on our way to the table.

"Rain, are you ready to head back to the room?"

Monica asked her friend, slipping her phone back into her bag. Rain shot her a teasing smirk and nodded, standing up to thank Jordan and me for the drinks.

I reached out, gently taking each of their hands and kissing the backs of them as they turned to leave.

"What did you two get up to?" Jordan asked, his eyebrow raised.

I glanced at Monica, her hips swaying just enough to drive me wild, and I felt a surge of desire to scoop her up and take her straight back to my hotel room.

"What did you two get up to?" I countered, patting his arm, which earned me an immediate middle finger in response.

"One for the road?" Jordan suggested, gesturing towards the bar.

I nodded in agreement. Approaching the bartender, I pointed to a whiskey sitting on the top shelf and raised two fingers. Jordan exhaled deeply as we slammed our glasses down on the bar, a satisfying thud echoing through the dimly lit room. He threw an arm around my shoulders as we made our way back to the suite.

"Night!" Jordan called as he entered his room.

"Night," I replied, already lost in my thoughts. As I began unbuttoning my shirt, the sweet scent of berries filled my nose. Monica had mentioned earlier that she would be leaving the day after tomorrow. Normally, I wouldn't bother asking for a number after a one-night stand, but a part of me wished I had asked for hers.

We woke up late in the afternoon, the sun filtering through the curtains as we lounged around, ordering room service to our heart's content. After bingeing on food and watching every Italian soap drama that Rome had to offer on the TV, the evening quickly rolled around. So, I jumped into the shower, my thoughts drifting to Monica—the way her body felt beneath mine, her soft skin, those perfect curves. The memory sent a rush through me, and I found myself responding to the fantasy. I reached down, pumping my dick and moaning her name as I reached my peak.

My jaw felt tense from gritting down my teeth. Once I rinsed off, the steam of the shower still lingering in the air, I turned off the water and stepped out, feeling refreshed. I quickly slipped into a pair of fresh clothes that clung comfortably to my skin, the fabric soft against me.

As I made my way to the kitchen, the familiar scent of coffee beans filled my senses, drawing me toward the island. I approached the coffee machine and, with a satisfying click, pressed the button for a double espresso. The machine whirred to life, and I watched as dark, rich liquid began to fill my cup, anticipation building with each drop.

"Want to go down to that bar again tonight?" Jordan asked, walking out of his room, and buttoning up his white shirt.

"Did something pique your interest last night?" I wiggled my eyebrows at him.

"Maybe. She was pretty cool, man." he mumbled looking down at his shirt. Was he going red? I wondered if Jordan asked Rain for her number.

"Did you get Rain's number?"

He waved a piece of paper at me. I take that as a yes. I reminded myself to swipe that piece of paper from him later.

After a minute he returned with his jacket. I slipped on my shoes and threw my own jacket on.

For the third night in a row, we made our way to the bar. We arrived around the same time, just like every night when I bumped into Monica. But a few hours had passed, there was no sign of Monica and

Rain and Jordan was starting to slur his words.

"Let's have another drink," Jordan slurred in between hiccups.

"No. Come on, let's get you back to the room" I replied, standing up from the bar stool. We entered the suite, and I threw Jordan onto his bed. I wasn't going to undress my big brother; he can do that himself.

•·················•·················•

The next morning, a bittersweet mix of excitement and reluctance filled the air as Jordan and I began repacking our suitcases, getting ready to leave this beautiful city behind for our flight home to Manchester. After a quick stop downstairs to return our keycards to the receptionist, we stepped out onto the bustling streets of Rome, the vibrant energy of the city wrapping around us. Jordan tapped on his phone and a black stretch limousine appeared from around the corner.

A short while later the limo pulled up to the airport, we grabbed our luggage from the back of the car, tipped the driver and headed inside towards check in.

A slim blonde with captivating blue eyes examined my passport, holding it just a second longer than necessary before handing it back with a playful smile.

"Have a safe flight, Mr. Marino," she purred, her gaze lingering as her lashes fluttered, clearly hoping I would notice.

I offered a polite, faint smile in response—on any

other day, I might have leaned into the moment, traded a few flirty lines. But today, it couldn't be less interested. Slipping my passport into my hand luggage, I headed toward the screens to find my gate. Jordan walked up beside me as I stood looking up.

"She was flirting with you by the way,"

"She wasn't my type"

I lied.

He hummed as I led the way to our departure gate. I thought this short trip would clear my mind, not add more chaos. All I could think about was the silkiness of Monica's hair slipping through my fingers, her warm scent filling the air between us. The way her skin responded to my touch, a trail of goosebumps rising with every gentle caress. I remembered how she bit her lip, stifling a laugh as her eyes held mine.

What were the chances of feeling her that close again?

8 MONICA

"Are you feeling better?" I asked Rain as I pulled the bed cover back over her.

Placing the back of my hand against her head, I could feel her burning up. Spotting her medicine bag across the room, I walked over to her dressing table and popped out two painkillers for her to take. Rain started to feel ill yesterday afternoon, as she often suffered from stomach flare ups, I knew she wouldn't feel up to going out. After years of an endless number of tests during high school, college, and university, they couldn't find anything wrong with her. In the end her parents put the flare ups down to stress.

So, she spent most of yesterday in bed, running a fever and taking naps. During high school If one of us had the day off school, the other would call in sick too and show up at their doorstep with movies, medicine, and junk food. She popped her head up from under the cover. "Yeah, I'm feeling a lot better. I'm sorry about cancelling last night."

I leaned down to stroke her hair.

"Don't be silly. We can go out any night. You just focus on feeling better."

She smiled and snuggled back into her pillow.

Our flight wasn't leaving until tomorrow afternoon, so I spent the day packing our clothes and toiletries into our suitcases. Rain started to fall asleep again, so I left two bottles of ice-cold water and some more painkillers on her bedside table. I closed the door to her room and made my way back to my own. Leaning against the door I glanced over at my suitcase that was sitting on the bed, waiting to be repacked. The sounds of people shouting and laughing in the street floated in through the window across the room.

That reminded me of my new apartment back home. I wanted one that specifically had a balcony. People watching was my favourite pastime, I often made up stories in my head of what their lives were like. When I went to view the apartment, I knew it would be perfect for me. Pushing myself off the door with my hands, I walked across the room, opened the wardrobe, and slipped my sparkly silver dress off the wooden clothes hanger. The fabric now smelled like Chase's cologne. My cheeks went warm at the memory of that night. At the sight of his eyes burning into me. His hands were all over me in the lift to his suite. His lips against my neck. What a perfect night with a perfect stranger.

Shaking my head, I folded my dress and placed it inside. I zipped up my case and leaned over the dressing table to grab my red lipstick. I have decided this little container was my good luck charm. I opened my carry-on bag and slipped it into one of the inside pockets.

•……………•……………•

The next morning, I made my way down in the lift, through reception and stepped out onto the lively street outside our hotel. A charming bakery caught my eye just a few doors down. As I pushed through the door, the sweet aroma of fresh pastries hit me, and the little bell above chimed softly, welcoming me inside. I picked out fresh cream cakes and picked up two espressos. Breakfast in hand I entered our hotel reception and pushed the call button for the lift. I walked down the corridor to Rain's room, taking a second to appreciate the paintings of different scenic spots of Rome on the walls. I brought my knuckles to the door and knocked twice. Rain answered the door, the colour had returned to her skin, and she no longer looked feverish.

"You look so much better today" I told her as I placed the pastries onto her dressing table.

"How could you say that." She placed her hand to her chest dramatically.

I rolled my eyes at her, "You know what I mean."

She let out a small giggle and shuffled over to me.

She opened the box of pastries and handed one to me. As I took a bite, Rain eyed me curiously.

"So, I didn't get a chance to ask—where did you and Chase disappear to?"

I turned to my best friend, swallowed my food, and told her every single detail. She raised her eyebrows and let out a soft gasp.

"Well, happy birthday indeed."

She wasn't wrong, it would be a birthday I'll never forget.

Later in the afternoon, we checked out of our rooms and headed to the airport. As we walked through the terminal, I remembered that I hadn't asked Rain about her night.

"What happened between you and the brother, by the way?"

She grabbed my arm, stopping me in my tracks.

"You mean the one who is standing right over there?"

I followed her gaze towards our gate, and before I could stop myself, we both burst into laughter. We quickly ducked behind a group of travellers just as Chase and Jordan turned around.

9 MONICA

"Okay, that's the last one," I told Skye, setting the cardboard box labelled 'Mugs & Shit' on the kitchen counter of my new apartment.

"Is Carlos still downstairs? I want to pop down and ask him something."

I nodded as Skye patted my arm on her way out of the door. She had been here all morning and most of this week —painting, hanging frames, putting up shelves. Yesterday, she and Rain had loaded up the moving truck, shuttling boxes from their parents' house to Rain's new place, which was conveniently just across the road from mine. Gently cradling the base, I carried the housewarming plant from Skye out to the balcony, the leaves brushing against my arm. I carefully placed it on the small metal table, hoping it would thrive in its new spot, just like I hoped to in mine. I started unpacking, carefully placing each of my mugs into the cupboard above the sink, their new home. As I lined them up, I couldn't help but feel a mix of excitement and mild panic—this was my space now. At least if everything else fell apart, I'd still have an army of mugs ready for emotional support (or excessive amounts of coffee). Shortly after the divorce my father sold the house I grew up in and moved into the living space above the pub.

Even though the pub was just a short drive from my dorm back then, I still missed being around him all the time. But having my own apartment now gives me a sense of independence. My plants and hand-painted mugs will have to keep me company from here on out. I opened the box labelled 'clothes' and pulled out a complete work outfit ready for tomorrow. My first day at my new job. As I unpack and hang up the rest of the clothes, I pull out my sparkly dress. This shall be known as my 'lucky' dress going forward, as well as my red lipstick, that seems to have gone missing again. Scoffing at myself for losing the lipstick, again, I pulled out my phone, searched up the brand's website and placed an order for ten more lipsticks.

"Knock, knock" Rain shouts from the open door, without knocking. I exited my room back into the living room and brought out my arms to give her a hug.

"Hey, how's it going? How's your new apartment?" I asked her, grabbing both large takeout coffee cups she held in her hands. I took a sip of the steaming hot beverage, walked over, and placed it onto the wooden coffee table. The apartment's living space and kitchen blended into one open room, creating a cosy but functional space. The bathroom and my bedroom were tucked just behind the closest door to the entryway, making everything feel compact yet perfectly laid out.

"All good, thank you. Skye bought me the most gorgeous plant and some new crystals."

She pulled out her phone and began swiping through some photos.

"I passed Skye on my way up and she told me to tell you that she would come back to yours later tonight."

"Oh okay, cool. Thanks for letting me know."

She settled onto the pale blue sofa I'd picked up from the second-hand shop down the street, its worn cushions soft but full of character, just like everything else in this place.

"I'm so excited for tomorrow. Text me as soon as you get into the office and when you meet your boss and the team."

Nodding my head I told her "Of course I will, make sure you do the same." She responded with a salute. I sat down next to her and switched on the TV. I joined her on the sofa and spent the next hour or so watching some silly cat videos on YouTube

"Did you get Chase's number, by the way?" she asked. I shook my head.

"Nope. Did you get Jordan's?" She shook her head too.

"I gave him my email instead." Email?

"Why your email?" I asked, raising an eyebrow.

"He said it's good to know someone who works in finance and likes money as much as he does." A laugh slipped out of me.

"What did you say to that?" I asked, flicking through the video suggestions on YouTube. She shrugged.

"I told him, 'I don't like money, I love money. That's why I work in finance.'" I grinned.

"Well, I hope he emails you—and throws in his brother's number at the end."

She let out a small giggle. Rain stayed at mine until late in the evening. We ordered a couple of pizzas, which were good but nowhere near as good as the ones we had in Rome and watched a cheesy romance film.

"Alright, it's home time for me," she said, rising from the sofa and planting a soft kiss on my cheek.

"Good luck tomorrow." I smiled as she pulled open the door.

"Same to you! Love you."

"Love you more," she called back, her voice fading as she walked down the corridor.

•···············•················•

My alarm buzzed on my phone the next morning. I reached over, groaned, and silenced my phone. I dragged my legs from the bed and stood to open the window. It was late August now, so the cool breeze in the morning refreshed the room as I began getting dressed for my first day at my new job. I switched on the radio, feeling in such a good mood I danced and sang whilst I ironed my white blouse and black pencil skirt. After watering my plants and pouring myself a cup of steaming hot coffee, I slipped into my loafers, threw on my black blazer, grabbed my bag and headed downstairs. On my way out, I spotted a familiar small black container sitting on my coffee table. I snatched it up and shoved it into my bag, fully convinced this lipstick grows legs and goes for a walkabout. My apartment was on the third floor, so the journey down the steps only took a few seconds. I walked through the main lobby area and headed for my car. My cherry red Ford Focus was parked round the back of the building in the resident's car park. I pulled the cold metal handle to the door and ducked inside. Before beginning my journey, I opened my phone to check my emails and found the message from Jane, the woman who interviewed me, including the address of the building. After our video interview, I was filled with excitement at the thought of finally seeing the place in person. I typed the address into the maps on my phone, clipped it onto the window-mounted stand, and turned the key in the ignition. That's when the car made a strange, unsettling sound. Please, not today. The engine spluttered for a few minutes before allowing me to pull off. I really needed to get a new car.

Twenty minutes later, I pulled into the car park in front of a towering stone building. Turning off the engine, I stepped out of the car and used the wing mirror to apply my 'lucky' lipstick. I reached over, grabbed my bag, and closed the door. Locking the car as I walked towards the huge main entrance of the building. I pushed through the shiny glass doors and was greeted by a familiar face waiting in reception—a woman about my height, with bottle-blonde hair. I stick out my slightly shaky palm to greet her formally.

"Hi Jane, it's so lovely to meet you in person."

She looked at me up and down before extending her hand out to shake my hand.

"Likewise, Miss Martinez, follow me please."

Hooking my bag onto my shoulder, I followed Jane into the lift and rode up to the tenth floor. During the ride up, she told me which floor the cafe, library and gym were and where my office would be.

"Mr. Marino owns the whole building. We have a wide range of businesses based here."

Jane explained as we walked out of the lift. My eyes landed on a huge red glowing sign that read 'Be Creative,' and something stirred inside me. The bold letters seemed to pulse with energy, like they were daring me to embrace the challenge ahead.

I let out a deep exhale as I once again followed Jane through a door that had 'Meeting Room' engraved onto it. We entered a huge room that had a cold drinks fridge in the corner, floor to ceiling windows and a black glass table that was surrounded with grey leather seats in the centre of the room. I pulled out a chair and sat down as the team went around the table, introducing themselves. From across the room, a tall, handsome man with a beard stood up. The room was full of beautiful people, and I would be lying if I said I wasn't feeling a bit intimidated. He walked over to me, extending a hand as he introduced himself.

"Hi Noah, it's nice to meet you."

My mouth was dry from the nerves, but I extended my hand and shook his hand.

Turning to the corner of the room towards the drink's fridge, he grabbed a cold bottle of water and placed it in front of me.

"Thank you," I said, twisting the cap open and taking a sip.

"No need to be nervous. What is the worst that could happen?" he chuckled softly, and I found myself relaxing. He was right—the job felt like an amazing opportunity for growth. The team was welcoming, and the building had everything I could need. Soon, the room buzzed with lively conversations and laughter as everyone eagerly swapped stories about their weekend adventures.

Everyone sat up straighter as the sound of heavy footsteps echoed down the corridor.

"Ready to meet the boss?" teased Chelsea, one of the assistants, flashing me a playful grin.

Out of the corner of my eye, I catch Jane tugging down her blouse, her pushed-up breasts instantly on display. The meeting room doors creaked open, and in walked...

No.

Noah was wrong. The worst had happened.

Chase.

10 CHASE

I pull into the car park at exactly eight AM. The car still reeks of the girl I picked up at the pub last night—Tiffany or Tina, I can't even remember. Her cheap perfume clings to the seats, a reminder that I need to get this car cleaned—or just scrap it altogether. Last night was supposed to be an escape, a release from all the tension I've been carrying. But it did nothing. She wasn't her. She didn't smell like sweet berries or have those seductive ruby-red lips. She was just there, in the right place at the wrong time. And now, that frustration I thought I'd left behind has returned. I'll work it off at the gym after work, or in the shower.

After a late-night tennis session with Jordan, we headed to one of our favourite spots—The Dog and Gun, a local pub we've grown pretty attached to.

It became our go-to when Jordan bought his first place, swearing he wouldn't live anywhere that didn't have a pub within a mile. We've been regulars ever since. The owner, who's now a good friend, always kicks off our nights by tempting us with a drink on the house. It has become our little tradition, a place to unwind and forget about everything else.

The night quickly wrapped up as Jordan downed a few brandies and ditched me, leaving me bored and frustrated, stuck with a girl who had been eyeing me all night. The evening ended with her giving me a blow job in my car, but I want a challenge.

Despite last night's event with that girl, I'm done with one-night stands.

My phone pings in my jacket pocket—an email from Jane. She's letting me know that the team, including the new hire, are already in the meeting room. I step out of the car and make my way to reception, pressing the call button for the lift. When the doors slide open, I'm greeted by one of my favourite sights in the entire building. It's the dream I started a decade ago, staring back at me in glowing red letters. With fingers tapping away on my phone, I scrolled through the hundreds of emails that were waiting for me after my return to Manchester. As I walked down the corridor toward the meeting room, I could hear the team clearing their throats and the conversation quieting down.

Eyes still glued to my phone, I pushed open the doors and took a seat at the top of the table.

"Good morning, Mr. Marino," my marketing manager Chelsea greets me, the team following.

"Good morn-."

Oh. Fuck. Am I dreaming? Or still slightly drunk from last night? Monica. She's here. At the table. Why didn't I check the name of the new hire? Why didn't Jane mention it? Probably because I never ask. It's not that I don't care—well, maybe I don't—but I trust Jane to handle them without any issues. Still.

She straightens her spine before opening those gorgeous ruby lips to speak.

"Hi, I'm Monica Martinez."

I love how she's acting like we haven't met before. Like, her name doesn't cross my mind a hundred times a day because I can't stop thinking about her. But hearing her voice again. It's like fucking music to my ears. She catches me glaring at her causing her cheeks to blush, almost matching her lipstick.

God, I love that shade of red.

"Good morning, Monica. I trust that the team has introduced themselves."

A humming sound rounds the team as they nod.

"Okay. Jane let's begin the induction presentation".

An hour of pure torture passed as I watched Monica's eyes flick between the screen and mine. Each time our gazes locked, she bit her lip, and I couldn't resist throwing her a cheeky wink. The sun shone through the floor to ceiling window, illuminating her raven black waves.

The moment the meeting ended, I shot up from my chair, eager to escape to my office. As I walk in with my back to the door, I hear heels click down the corridor, enter my office, and close the door.

I spot her reflection in the glass of the window before I turn around slowly.

"Hi" she says playfully.

It's taking everything in me not to throw her down on my desk and fuck her like I should have done that night.

"Hey, how have you been?" I give her body a quick glance.

"Good, you?" She shifts her eyes behind me as she begins to speak again, but I cut her off.

"I didn't see you at the bar, the night after."

Her eyes shift around the room. A nervous giggle escapes her mouth. I love the effect that I have on her. I'm starting to like the effect she has on me. She puckers her mouth, and I imagine what her lips would look like wrapped around my cock.

"Rain got sick, so we stayed at the hotel. Best friend duties and all that," she waves her hand around. I give her a small nod. The small pang of jealousy I had slipped away, I couldn't bear the thought of her with someone else engaging in another round of birthday celebrations. I step forward as she backs away, her hand rising in a halting gesture. I freeze in place.

"Chase. Look."

She lets out a shaky breath.

"I had fun in Italy, I really did. But we need to keep things professional," Monica says, crossing her arms. "If we start something, the whole team is going to think that I'm just doing it to make my way up in the business."

The team wouldn't think that in a million years, neither would I. I'm not having it. I take a step closer, my fingers slipping into her soft, thick hair as I gently tuck it behind her shoulder. My touch grazes her neck, and her chest rises with a sharp intake of breath.

"Okay."

Her eyes go wide at my response.

"But I wonder how long you'll last, Cherry."

I tower over her, and she gazes up, shaking her head and letting out a nervous laugh. It's as if she is trying to convince herself, rather than me, to keep things professional. I step back, creating some space between us, but she quickly reaches for the door handle and practically bolts out of my office and races down the corridor.

That is what I have been missing. Something to challenge me.

After meeting Monica, I am starting to think my parents might be right. Monica had passion and had an unforgettable laugh. I found her nervousness so damn sexy.

This is going to be fun.

11 MONICA

I don't think I've ever run out of a room so fast. Actually, I don't think I've ever run at all.

By the time I close the door to my office, I'm a little out of breath.

Or maybe that's just the effect Chase has on me. God, he looked so good in that suit—the way he stalked towards me, like a lion hunting its prey.

I sink into my chair and pull out my phone to text Rain, because of course she needs to hear how my day is going so far.

Me:

I slept with the boss...sort of

Rain (Bestie):

Already? Girl, that was fast ••

Me:

No, seriously. Guess who my boss is?

Me:

Chase...

Rain (Bestie):

NO FREAKING WAY!!
I'm rolling around on the floor

I'm glad she finds it so funny. I slam my phone down on my desk and put my head in my hands. A sound escapes me, I am not entirely sure if I am laughing or crying. During my induction, the IT team set up my laptop and office phone. I bring my head up from my hands and see Chase's number is at the top of the phone list. I could easily give in to his temptation. Resisting the urge, I exit my office and head towards the women's bathroom.

Jane is standing applying gloss in the mirror. I mimic her action and reapply my own lipstick.

"How's your first day going?" she asks, turning to look me up and down.

Have I done something to upset her?

"Good, thank you," I reply, shifting my gaze towards her as she opens her mouth.

"I noticed the way Mr. Marino was looking at you. Don't get your hopes up; he looks at all the new girls like that." Okay, that was slightly uncalled for.

"Chase-" I begin, but she coughs, clearly annoyed.

"Sorry. Mr. Marino I mean. Was just smiling at me. I'm sure he was just being polite. I'm not sure what you think you saw."

She slips her lip gloss into her pocket and storms out of the bathroom. Great, now I have royally pissed her off. Can I go back to bed yet?

The end of the day comes around and I have managed to avoid Chase and Jane for the last few hours. As I begin powering down my computer, there's a knock at my door. I lift my head to see him standing at my door.

He holds his hands up in defence.

"I come in peace. I just wanted to see if you wanted to grab a drink after work? Jordan will be there too, strictly professional" he leans against the doorframe, crossing his arms.

During my tour of the building, Jane did tell me how the company has some silent investors, I'm now guessing that Jordan is one of them. For a split second I consider his proposal.

"No thank you, I'm meeting Rain for dinner," I reply standing up from my chair. I pick up my jacket and pull my arms through the sleeves. Chase walks over and untucks my hair from the fabric. I whisper a thank you.

"Okay, if I can't change your mind, I'll leave to enjoy your evening."

With that he taps the top of the doorframe and walks backwards out of my office. Is it bad of me to wish that he wouldn't take no for an answer? A deep sigh escapes my body, and I close the glass door to my office and head towards the lift.

I enter my car, and my pocket vibrates with a message from my best friend. A smile tugs my lips as I look at the selfie of her and my dad, sticking their tongues out, which brightens my mood. I fire off a text telling her that I'm on my way.

Moving to my new apartment had taken up so many of my evenings this week, I barely had time to have dinner with my dad. When he picked me and Rain up from the airport, we told him all about our trip. Minus my 'birthday celebration' with Chase. The minute we stepped into the pub, he stuck the magnet I got him from Rome onto the bar fridge.

Traffic is light this time of the day, as I cruise down the high street to the pub. I pull into the car park, which is round the back of the pub, exit the car, and lock the doors. The strange noise my car made this morning hasn't repeated itself on my drive over. I make a mental note to visit a car dealership.

Rain is seated at the bar, enjoying a veggie burger and crispy French fries while sipping from a beautifully rich glass of red wine. I catch a glimpse of my dad leaning casually against the wall, where my high school awards and university graduation cap sit proudly on a nearby shelf. Just as I'm about to speak, he sets a glass down on the bar and begins to fill it, a knowing smile on his face.

"Only one muñeca, you're driving" he tells me, sliding the glass across to me as I take a seat on the wooden stool next to Rain. I give her a quick kiss on the cheek before stealing a French fry from her plate.

"Yes, father. I did drive here by the way," I threw some sass his way.

"I know, mi amor. I just want you to be safe." I lean over the bar and place a kiss on his stubbled cheek.

"How was your first day?" he asks whilst pulling a pint of beer for a customer. Rain sniggers next to me; I roll my eyes at her. "It was interesting, but the team is really nice."

My dad begins to speak but a voice distracts him, as someone enters through the main wooden doors behind me. You have got to be kidding me.

"Carlos, my man. How are you?" Chase extends his hand over the bar to shake my dad's hand.

What the hell is he doing here? Chase turns to me, his brother walking up behind him. Since when do they drink in this pub?

"What are you doing here?" I ask, snapping slightly.

"Mon don't be rude. Chase and his brother are some of my favourite customers. How do you know Chase?" My dad raises his eyebrows. Chase opens his mouth, but I interrupt him—something he loves to do to me.

"Chase is my boss, Dad." Jordan bursts out laughing and sneakily moves to sit next to Rain. I want the ground to open and swallow me whole. Chase turns to walk away, but not before placing his warm hard hand on my lower back, causing sparks to shoot up my spine.

"Ladies, I'll leave you to enjoy your wine."

He throws me a wink over his shoulder as he grabs Jordan and heads to a corner of the pub. Rain rapidly taps my arm, her chest vibrating with laughter. My cheeks warm as I shake my head. Meanwhile, my dad, still looking confused, leaves us to serve customers at the end of the bar.

The kitchen doors open from behind the bar and one of the kitchen staff places a plate of food in front of me, and I dig in. Conscious that Chase is watching me, I try to resist scanning the pub for him.

After we finish our food and drinks, Rain rises from her stool, her eyes sparkling.

"I need to swing by Lee and Aurora's to pick up some things I left behind," she says, zipping up her puffy purple coat with a playful grin. I don't think I'll ever get used to her calling her parents by their first names. Growing up, Lee and Aurora told their daughters they didn't mind being called Mum and Dad or by their first names.

They live a very free-flowing lifestyle, which I love for them, but I just can't imagine calling my dad by his name.

"Tell them both I said hi."

I bring her in for a hug and she waves before heading out of the main door. Feeling the day's events, I give my dad a hug too before heading to my car. My hand digs around in my bag as I look for my keys.

A heavy presence surrounds me as I unlock my car, then there's a weight pressing against my back. I exhale deeply, trying to steady my racing heart.

"What are you still doing here, Chase?" I ask, turning on my heels to face him.

A mischievous smirk spreads across his face, showing his features in a way that draws me in.

"Jordan got drunk, so I tossed him in a taxi," he says, swaying back and forth on the heels of his shoes, hands casually tucked in his pockets.

I glance down at my shoes, desperately trying to avoid the pull of his intoxicating gaze.

But before I can gather my thoughts, he lifts my chin, and my eyes lock with his. His touch is soft yet demanding, sending a shiver down my spine. In that moment, I find myself teetering on the edge, struggling to resist the magnetic pull of his charm.

It's becoming increasingly difficult not to fall for the temptation. He begins to pepper small kisses over my jaw. "We're supposed to be keeping things professional" I whisper to him.

He moans against my ear,

"But we're not in the office now Cherry."

My knees buckle at his nickname for me. I allow myself a short amount of time, of his touching, his presence near me, a few seconds to inhale his aftershave. I tug at the sleeves of his jacket, and he pulls away.

He steps back and smirks before heading towards his car.

I watch him drive off, the sound of his engine revving as he speeds away. In a rush, I jump into my car, jamming the key into the ignition. Of course, it refuses to start. I let my head drop onto the steering wheel with a groan.

Just what I needed to top off this *fabulous* day.

12 CHASE

The coffee machine whirs inside the meeting room, as I press the button for a double espresso. I check the clock and a few minutes pass, and Monica is late. I grab my coffee and head to the meeting room, glancing at my watch every few seconds.

If she's thinking of quitting, I'll march down to her apartment and drag her here myself. I take a seat alongside my team for the morning briefing.

The doors swing open, and she comes flying into the room.

"Sorry I'm late. My car broke down last night and I had to grab an Uber," Monica says, breezing past me to grab a seat at the table. I give her a small nod and a wink. As Jane kicks off the meeting, I discreetly pull out my phone to text Jordan.

Me:

I need you to drop off a red Porsche 911 to the office.

Jordan (Dickhead):

Does this have anything to do with Monica's car that is still stranded in the pub car park?

Jordan (Dickhead):

Saw it this morning when I went in to grab my jacket.

Me:

Maybe...

Jordan (Dickhead):

You're unbelievable. I'll get it to you by the end of the day, Your Highness.

I slip my phone back into my pocket as the briefing wraps up and the team begins to shuffle out. "Monica, a moment, please," I say, catching her attention. The sun beams through the window just as she turns. Her eye colour changes from a deep brown to a soft caramel colour in the strobes of light. Once again, I'm lost in them, lost in the memory of that night. She rocks on the balls of her feet and clears her throat softly, bringing my attention back.

"I'll need you to come with me to visit a client in a few days," I add, watching her eyes widen.

"It's a big client—one you'll be handling. The meetings in London, so we'll need to stay overnight." Her arms cross, and I can see her mind working behind that concerned expression. I know what she's thinking, despite how feral I am to get her back into a hotel room with me, I also want to make her happy.

"Separate rooms, of course," I add, taking a small step closer.

"Okay. Send me all the details" she replies, before turning to leave, hips swaying as she walks out of the room. I catch myself multiple times a day watching her as she goes about her day, walking back and forth between her office, to the meeting room, to the kitchen, her tight clothing sitting perfectly on her soft curves. I'm probably coming off as a full-on creep, but damn, it's hard to look away.

I walk over to the drinks fridge and grab myself a cold bottle of water. Right now, I need a cold fucking shower.

My thoughts drift to Rome, to the heat of that night, to the sound of her pussy when I was pumping my fingers inside her. I let out a breath, thankful I'm alone right now, because the memory of her thighs is doing things to me.

Later that day, as I walk past her office, I catch the sound of her voice on a video call with clients. There's a confidence in her tone that I can't help but admire. Curious, I peek through the office window. She's gesturing animatedly, discussing project plans with the kind of focus that's hard to ignore.

I've always appreciated people who are passionate about their work, and seeing her like this, it strikes me—Monica isn't just talented, she's got that drive, the fire I look for. Someone who doesn't hold back. It hits me that, in so many ways, she's the kind of woman who could even keep up with me. I get lost in a daydream, imagining one day making Monica an official business partner. The thought of working side by side with her every day, sharing ideas, and building something together—it sounds like pure bliss.

Just as I start to lose myself in the fantasy, Jane pops her head into my office, breaking the spell.

"Your brother's waiting downstairs," she says, a knowing look on her face.

I grunt a quick thanks and head for the lift. A few moments later, I'm walking across the busy reception area, scanning the room for Jordan. I spot him, leaning against the counter, looking like he owns the place.

I pull him in for a handshake hug, feeling the familiar weight of his grip. He hands me the keys to the car, and I slip them into my pocket.

We head outside to the car park so I can take a quick walk around the car, checking every detail to make sure it's perfect for Monica.

Jordan raises an eyebrow, a mischievous grin spreading across his face.

"Maybe she'll find a way to thank you for the car," he says, wiggling his eyebrows exaggeratedly.

I roll my eyes, a smile tugging at the corners of my mouth, and give him a light punch on the shoulder. "Shut up, idiot," I mutter, but there's no hiding the fact that his teasing has got me thinking.

Jordan laughs, completely unbothered.

Me and Jordan wrestled a lot as kids, so he can handle a few punches and elbows to the ribs now. I shake his hand as he enters a car driven by one of his colleagues and heads back to the dealership. I fired off an email to Monica asking her to meet me downstairs.

My feet bounced slightly at the excitement of seeing her. Her eyes meet mine as she strolls over to me, and her new car. She doesn't need to know that it's not a company car. It's hers now.

"You wanted to see me, Mr. Marino?" Monica asks, her gaze flicking towards the car.

Her mouth opens slightly in surprise.

"Nice car is it yours?".

She cups her hands around her eyes, peering through the driver's side window. I pull the keys from my pocket, dangling them in front of her like a toy teasing a cat.

"It's yours." Her eyes widened.

"But my car—" she starts, clearly confused.

"Jordan's taken care of it," I cut in smoothly.

She reaches up for the keys, but I lift them just out of reach.

"And call me Chase when no one's around. I like how my name sounds on your lips."

Monica bites her lower lip, glaring up at me before nodding. I hand over the keys, stepping back to enjoy the sight of her bending down to open the door.

"I can't believe I've got a Porsche!" she squeals. I lean against the top of the car and whisper, "Anything you want, Cherry." I murmur under my breath. My gaze flicks to the slight movement as she squeezes her thighs together, and I can't help but smirk.

•················•················•

After spending all day in my office thinking about how Monica was only a few doors down, I headed home to change into my football kit and met up with Jordan for a late-night kickabout at the local field. I didn't hold back, sending the ball flying toward him with a solid kick.

"Oi, what's got into you?" Jordan laughs, barely stopping the ball.

"And why are you smiling like you've just won the lottery?".

"I'm just in a good mood, that's all," I say, trying to play it cool, even though I know my grin's giving me away. Jordan narrows his eyes as he kicks the ball back.

"Good mood? You? It's a girl, isn't it? No—wait. It's Monica."

I laugh, running up to tackle him but I trip slightly causing a curse to escape my lips. I turn my head towards Jordan.

"Who says it's about her?".

"Come on, I'm not blind," he shoots back, trying to shake me off. "You've got that look—the 'I'm going to have some fun chasing her' look." He nudges my shoulder with his own as we pass the ball to each other.

"Maybe I am," I say, flashing him a cocky grin.

Truth is, I can't stop thinking about her. She doesn't know about my past—and she doesn't need to. I wouldn't do that to her. The thought of fucking and ditching her tugs at something in my chest.

Jordan groans, kicking the ball between his feet.

"Just don't mess it up, yeah? She's got to survive working with you."

"Hey! I'm a delight to work with!" I retort, laughing as I steal the ball.

13 MONICA

I drive my car to my apartment, bursting with excitement. I texted Rain before I left the office, telling her to wait in the car park so I could show her my new wheels. Her jaw drops as I pull in. "No fucking way!" she screams as I step out of the car. She walks around the car, copying my action from earlier, cupping her hands over her eyes and peering inside. Rain puts her lips together and blows out a wolf whistle.

"Come on, I'll take you for a spin", I open the door and gesture to her to take a seat inside. I slip into the driver's seat and start up the beast.

"What happened to your car?" she asks, opening the glove compartment and pulling out some paperwork.

"It broke down outside the pub last night." She stares at me with compassion; she knows I loved that car. "So, Jordan had it scrapped, and then Chase gave me a Porsche."

She lets out a throaty laugh, sliding the unread paperwork back into the glove box. We fasten our seatbelts, and I push the button to start the car. As we turn to look at each other, our eyes meet, and we both squeal at the engine's deep, thrilling rumble.

We walk through the door of our local Italian restaurant, Sogno Italiano (Italian Dream), and are shown to a table. I stare at the menu even though I know I'm going to order the same thing I order every time.

"I'll have the pesto pasta" I hand the menu back to the waiter.

"I'll have the same. Thank you". Rain repeats the same action. She places her elbows on the table and rests her head on her hands. I eye her suspiciously.

"So, any secret late night office sex with Chase yet?". I burst out laughing, covering my hands with my mouth.

"Rain. Hell no." But I don't tell her how many times I thought something would happen. One night, after everyone had gone home, I stayed late at the office, sending emails to new clients. I headed to the staff kitchen to make myself a coffee, only to find Chase standing there doing the same thing. Our hands would brush as we reached for the coffee pot, causing sparks to shoot across my skin. He'd give me a sly smile before walking out. Leaving me a hot mess in the kitchen.

But I do tell her about my upcoming trip with him.

"Oh, I wonder if you'll have sex in the hotel".

"Rain, what's gotten into you?" I giggle as she takes a sip from her glass of wine as I take a sip from mine.

"Jordan's been texting me all week and he has…erm… a very sexual sense of humour. He constantly sends me these hilarious memes. I think they're rubbing off on me".

I shake my head, laughing.

"Maybe his brother will start rubbing off on you", she wiggles her eyebrows at me as I roll my eyes.

I kind of hope he does. *Stop Monica, that's the wine talking.*

The same waiter brings out our food a short while after and we begin catching up on things that are happening rather than mentioning certain things that should not happen.

"How's Skye, by the way? She seemed really upset one morning when she was decorating."

She threw her paintbrush across the room after getting a call from her husband.

I take a bite of my delicious pasta, waiting for Rain's answer. She sets her fork down on the table. "Her and Steve have been arguing a lot recently."

She rolls her eyes; she's never been the biggest fan of Steve. They got married a year ago after being together for six months. They seemed so in love. Skye and Steve began their relationship as business partners, but I get the feeling he never really got the hang of balancing being both a husband and a business partner. It hurts a little because I love Rain and Skye as much as I would if they were my biological sisters. I carry on eating, as Rain continues.

"He makes decisions without her. It's her company too. I wouldn't be completely upset if they split up one day". That causes me to choke on my food a little. I pick up my wine and take a sip, the liquid instantly cooling my throat.

"Why would you say that?".

She lets out a deep sigh, "because my sister deserves way better". I'm not going to argue with her, I think I agree.

I drop Rain off at her apartment before pulling into the car park of mine. My feet instantly feel free and have some sensation returning to them, after kicking off my high heels. I fill a small cup of water for my plant, grab my phone from my bag, pour a glass of wine, and juggle all three as I take a seat at the blue metal table on my balcony. My plant and I are feeling very refreshed. For the next thirty minutes or so I scroll through lingerie websites. I have time to focus on other things now other than university and finding a job, maybe I should shift my focus onto dating for a while. *Not Chase though. Monica do not date your boss.* I give in and place an order for a gorgeous, lace ruby red matching bra and thong set. Chuckling to myself, for ordering underwear that matches the colour of my new car. And that probably matches the colour that my cheeks go every time I see Chase. Why does he have to be so hot? Its torture being around him. He's the perfect deadly combination of sexy, sweet and slightly possessive. I down the rest of my wine and go to bed. Before I do something stupid, *like call Chase.*

My alarm buzzes the next morning, and I drag myself to the gym at the office for a workout. It's quiet for a Saturday, which suits me just fine. Before my workout, I stop by the café and order a green smoothie. I'm trying to be healthy, especially after the copious amounts of wine I've downed this week. One sip in, and I'm fighting the urge to gag. Why do people willingly drink this instead of wine? Oh, right—because it's *good* for you. I'm trying to embrace new things, after all. I even downloaded a dating app this morning. Then promptly deleted it about as fast as I tossed this disgusting smoothie in the bin.

As I scanned my company card to enter the gym, I expected to see Jane here, maybe in some ridiculously high cut shorts and a revealing top. She blows hot and cold with me at the office most days. I can't help but wonder if there is some history between her and Chase. The way she acts around him makes me think there could be. I wouldn't blame her for at least trying.

I look around the gym and there are a few people using the machines that I don't recognise, I'm assuming they're from the other businesses in the building. I head to the locker room and shove my bag and shoes into a free locker. After an hour of cardio, I decided to warm my skin in the sauna before going back outside into the cold. It's almost autumn now, and the air carries a crisp chill in the early hours of the morning. Closing my eyes and tipping my head back, I will myself to relax. The sound of the sauna door closing forces me to open my eyes. I trail the length of his body, taking my time to stare at his toned legs, his abs, his chest that's covered in tattoos to meet his gaze.

"Are you following me, Cherry?" he asks, taking a seat on the bench above me. I spread my hands out on my thighs as the moisture in the air causes my hands to become clammy.

"Nope" I tell him, popping the P. "Just a coincidence".

He just hums in response. It's been five painfully long minutes since Chase entered the sauna and the silence is killing me. I open my mouth to speak as he lowers himself next to me. Before my brain can process what is happening, Chase swings my legs around his waist. His hands roam across my chest as he hooks my arms around his neck. His breath his warm across my lips as he closes the space between us. He runs his tongue across his lips, which causes me to bite my lower lip.

"It kills me when you bite your lip like that Monica" he runs his thumb across my lower lip. I ignore his tease, even if it does cause my core to throb. I bring down my hands and begin to trace the tattoos on his chest.

"What do your tattoos mean?" I trace my fingers over the inky swirls, following the curves like they hold a secret.

"That some pain is worth enduring if it leads to something beautiful."

He shifts his eyes from my chest to meet my eyes. He has a twinkle in his eyes, that I'm not sure was there the night I met him. For a second, I think we could work. For a split second I see a happily ever after for us.

I snap out of this trance that Chase has me in. I drop my head to his chest and let out a small giggle.

Using the bench behind Chase, I push myself and climb off his lap, which causes a look of confusion to grow across his face.

"See you on Monday, Mr Marino" are my last words before closing the door to the sauna and walking away.

That was *way* too close.

14 CHASE

Monica leaves me high and dry in the sauna, so I wait a few minutes before leaving, her grinding on me leaves me with the biggest hard-on since that night in Rome. Closing the glass door, I head to the showers to wash and get dressed. Since I'm already in the office, I head upstairs to organise travel and accommodation for mine and Monica's trip that's coming up in a few weeks. As I shut down my laptop, my phone pings in the pocket of my jacket.

Jordan (Dickhead):

Drink tonight? Usual place

Me:

Sure. Meet you there at seven.

Jordan (Dickhead):

I'll save you a seat next to Monica.

Me:

I pull into the pub car park of my new favourite spot. Carlos and I go back about a year now since Jordan moved into the apartment a few roads down from here, and though I don't know all the details, I know enough to admire him. He once told me how his wife walked out on him and their daughter ten years ago and that he was basically raising the kid on his own. I just wish he introduced me to Monica sooner, but I won't hold that against him. The guy's a rock, and I respect him more than I can say. He's the kind of father I hope to be one day. *Wait, since when did I start thinking about fatherhood?* Seriously, what's happening to me? This girl's got me all twisted up. More than I realised. I said to myself that I wouldn't get involved with women I work with, but Monica is irresistible.

Thinking about Carlos, has me remembering how much I'm missing my parents. Jordan walks out to meet me in the car park.

As he walks over to me I pull out my phone and video call them. Jordan waves into the camera as my parents blow kisses through the camera.

"We miss you! Come visit us in Verona". Jordan and I share a look.

We both know she is just going to ask a million questions about when we're both going to settle down. However, Jordan and I have a little deal. We take our deals seriously—after all, as siblings, we do everything together. We started our businesses at the same time, had our first legal drink together, and even got into trouble together more times than I can count. He's always been my partner in crime, whether we were sneaking out as teenagers or pulling all-nighters to make sure our ventures didn't crash and burn.

We've had each other's backs through every major milestone, and now, here we are, navigating adulthood with the same intensity. This deal? Just another chapter in the long book of our sibling escapades. If anything, it makes the competition between us even more fun. Because let's be real—bragging rights are everything in this family.

I bring my attention back to our mother as she screams down the phone.

"Bring your girlfriends".

Ah, there it is.

"We'll think about it", she rolls her eyes at me. We catch up on a few other things during the call.

"Ti voglio bene, mamma." She blows kisses down the phone as I tell her I love her, before ending the call.

I turn to my brother "Let's go get that drink". He responded by giving me a pat on the shoulder.

We start the night off easy, beers followed by a few glasses of whiskey. Jordan deals out the cards on the wooden table as I tell him about mine and Monica's plans to visit our new client.

"There's a really nice restaurant down the road from that hotel, you know" he gives me a wink as he passes me my hand of cards. I place the first card down to start the game.

"And, what?" I roll my eyes at him.

"You could get a few drinks with Monica, since you're staying together". He throws down a card, I collect one.

"In separate rooms. To keep things professional". He blinks at me.

"If it's what she wants, I'm happy with that". He blinks at me again, as if he doesn't believe me. I'm not sure I believe me. But I do want to make her happy. Especially if it makes her smile more. Her smile and laugh do things to me, as well as when she sways her hips as she walks away from me. I'm sure she does that deliberately. After a few rounds of cards and drinks, which is one of our favourite things to do on a Saturday night, we both called it a night and split a taxi back to our apartments.

As I walk into my apartment, my phone pings with a message from my web designer Noah.

I send my reply but before I exit my company's messaging software, I look at the chat below Noah's and see that Monica is online. It's almost eleven at night and she's still working. *She might just work harder than me.* That tight feeling in my chest returns. I quickly change her name to her nickname; she won't be able to see the change, but I'll be able to see it from my side.

Me:

You work almost as much as I do Cherry ♡

Cherry:

I most certainly do, Mr Marino ♡

Me:

What are you wearing?

Me:

Sorry, auto correct. I meant to say writing.

Cherry:

I'm writing a business proposal for our new client.

Cherry:

And I'm not wearing anything...

I request to switch to video call. She accepts. She answers and she's wearing her dressing gown. Her laugh travels down the video call which causes me to laugh.

"Good night, Mr Marino".

"Wait." I lean forward a little, so I have a better angle of her perky tits.

"Take off the dressing gown".

She begins to slowly remove the fabric, sliding it down her shoulders to reveal a red strap. The phone goes black, or did I black out? Nope. She ended the call.

It's at that moment I realise that I have finally met my match. I went to sleep that night smiling like a fool.

Monday morning rolls around and I enter Monica's office to place some files on her desk for when she arrives. I also leave her a note telling her to meet me in my office after the workday ends. I go about my day, responding to emails and attending meetings with my team. In a good mood, I challenged Noah to a game of tennis at the gym towards the end of the day. Noah's a great guy—he's been with the company for about five years, designing and developing websites. The guy's fitness-obsessed and trains for marathons in his spare time, which is probably why he ended up beating me. Not something that usually happens. Clearly, I'm off my game today.

After a quick shower, I get dressed in a white shirt and navy trousers before heading back to my office. Monica is standing by the window, her back to me, gazing out at the city lights.

"Hey", she spins on her heels to greet me.

I'm not sure if I love looking more at the back or front of her.

"Hey", I place my phone and bag onto my desk. "I just wanted to confirm all the details for the meeting in a few weeks", she takes a step closer to me.

"Okay." she almost whispers. I take her hand in mine and I can see her eyes are slightly glassy. My chest suddenly feels tight, I will hurt anyone that upsets her.

"Everything okay?" I whisper to her. She turns to face me.

"Tomorrow is my dad's birthday-" she breathes out and then in again, "and he's going on a date. I know he and my mother split up a long time ago, but it feels strange that he's dating another woman. I do want him to be happy, my mother never made him happy. I'm guessing because you and my dad are such good friends you know about our past".

Her voice has a bite to it. She shakes her head at me, "Sorry. I don't mean to be so depressing".

She lets out a nervous laugh. I lift her chin, so she stares up at me.

"Don't apologise. Carlos is a great guy; he deserves to be happy. You both do. I know about your past and I also know that your mother didn't deserve either of you".

She smiles up at me and nods her head in agreement.

I stroke my hand down her arm as she plays with the sleeves of my jacket. I lean forward as she stands on the tips of her heels. My lips brush against hers and I drag my thumb across her jaw. Someone coughs as they walk into my office. *Fucking Jane.* We both jump at the sound and move apart from each other. Jane eyes up Monica as she walks over and places some files onto my desk.

"Your reports, Mr Marino".

I pick up the files that are so fucking important that Jane had to interrupt.

"Thank you, Jane, can you close the door on your way out please?".

She flicks her tongue against the side of her mouth as she storms out of my office. I take slow steps towards Monica. She lets out a deep breath and a giggle. I bring her in for a hug and she nuzzles my neck. The girl has made me soft; I swear.

For the next few weeks, I'm out of the office, meeting clients and catching up with my external PR team. *And missing seeing Monica's face every day.* But tonight, I'm sitting across from Tom Hadley, the head of the team, at a local bar. As I set two pints of beer on the table, I noticed the sticky surface pulling at the edges of his notepad, making the paper cling to the wood. *I miss The Dog and Gun.*

"So, what's the latest with the award shows and press releases, Tom?" I ask, leaning back in my chair. He clears his throat, glancing at his notes.

"We've got the 'Business of the Year' award coming up in a few months. This year, it's in Paris." A smirk tugs at my lips. Paris means a weekend-long trip—with Monica. Tom continues.

"Your silent investors will be there too, assuming you win, they'll back the expansion plans for the Australia office next year." He raises an eyebrow, waiting for my reaction.

No pressure, right? I chuckle, leaning forward.

"No problem. We've got a strong team now—we'll win."

I lift my glass, taking a sip, but notice my hand's trembling slightly. Whether it's excitement or nerves, I can't quite tell.

15 MONICA

"No, not that one. Wear this one".

Rain walks over to my wardrobe and picks out my sparkly silver dress. She wiggles her eyebrows at me. The weeks flew by and my trip to London had quickly approached. So, I asked Rain to come over and help me pick an outfit for my trip. I grabbed the dress from her hands and hung it back in the wardrobe. I shake my head at her.

"Nopc, I'm wearing this one".

I show her a red dress that has long sleeves and would do nothing for my tits or curves. *But it's professional.* I let out a huff as she giggled at me. I give her a small giggle back.

With my small weekend bag packed, I swipe a bottle of white wine from the fridge and pour two glasses for us.

I join Rain on my sofa and pull my phone out of my pocket.

"So, how's things with Rain?" I ask her as I switch on my Sony speaker and load up a playlist.

"Rain is fine, my new job is great". She lets out a little sigh.

"But, coming back to a quiet apartment every night is getting a bit lonely".

My neck strains a little from how fast I turn to face her.

"Are you finally ready for a boyfriend?". She picks at her pink nail polish and shrugs.

"I think so, yes. Either that or a cat".

A laugh bubbles out of us. Knowing Rain, she'd prefer a cat. They cause way less heartbreak than men.

I scroll through my music app, searching for the perfect playlist as Rain keeps talking.

"It would be nice to finally—" she waves her hand vaguely in the air, trailing off.

"To finally what?" I glance up from my phone, confused.

"Rain, are you—?" Before I can finish, she snatches the phone from my hand.

"Oh look, I love this song," she says, quickly picking a track I'm pretty sure she's never heard before.

She hides her face behind her hands but peeks at me through parted fingers. I give her a playful grin and mime locking my lips, and she smiles back, the tension easing just a bit. I'll leave that conversation for another day.

Rain's short legs and my long legs are tangled up as I wake up and realise that we fell asleep cuddled up on the sofa after watching a film. The sound of my phone buzzing wakes me up. I look over to see Rain is still sleeping. A smile forms on my face as I stare down at the screen.

Unknown:

Text me your address

Unknown:

It's Chase

I sent him my address and saved his number in my contacts.

Mr Marino:

Thanks Cherry, see you at 7am

Me:

Setting my phone face down on the table, I attempt to drift back to sleep, but it buzzes once more.

Mr Marino:

Are you alone...?

Before I can reply to his text, my phone buzzes in my hand—he's calling. Trying to keep the noise down, I slip into my bedroom and answer.

"Hey, what are you up to?" His deep voice sends a shiver down my spine.

"Just in my room, going over notes for tomorrow." I have no idea why I lied, but I'm curious about why he called. He chuckles, low and warm.

"You're a terrible liar. I can hear the TV in the background." I glance at Rain, still fast asleep on the couch, then quietly close the door behind me. Falling back onto my bed, I bite my lip.

"Okay, you caught me. I was just about to hop in the shower and head to bed."

Another lie. His voice drops, darker and more tempting.

"Let me help with that." A thrill runs through me at the change in his tone.

Hang up.

Do not carry on the phone call.

Hang up the phone.

Don't say another word.

He's drunk and is looking for a quick phone booty call.

"Okay, Mr. Marino," I responded, slow and teasing, ignoring my inner thoughts. He always brings out this side of me, the one that leaves my skin tingling and my heart racing.

"Remove your top," Chase says through gritted teeth. I place my phone onto my black cotton sheets to follow his order. Removing the fabric causes my body temperature to rise instead of dropping. "Okay, done" I place the phone back to my ear.

"Now, your bottoms". Using my shoulder to trap my phone to my ear, I slip off my jeans.

"Next" I whisper down the phone.

“So eager Cherry”, he tuts down the phone. I roll my eyes as if he can see.

“Now your bra”. My nipples are already standing at peaks as I slip the black lace down my arm, trap the phone again and repeat the same for the other strap.

“Okay, done”, I whisper again. He moans and it makes my core throb. *Is he…?*

I build up the courage to ask but he sends another order down the line.

“Stick two fingers into your mouth and slide them down to your pussy”.

I’m not sure why I obey but when he speaks, I can’t help but follow. Using my left hand, I hold the phone to my ear and trail my fingers from my mouth down to my pussy with my other.

“Dip your fingers inside, bring them out and circle your clit”.

I begin the action, and a gasp escape my lips.

“Keep going Cherry, I’m right there with you” Chase coaxes me.

God, I wish it was his fingers and hands all over my body. I can hear his grunts becoming more rapid as my breathing gets faster. My core painfully throbs for a release. We both moan into each other's ears down the phone.

My legs tremble as I climax and hear Chase follow. Bringing my now shaky hand to the screen, I whisper down the phone.

“See you tomorrow, Mr Marino” and end the call. Using my arm to cover my face, I let out a deep groan.

Oh god. I just had phone sex with my boss.

After stepping out of the bathroom, to wash away the embarrassment off my hands, I quickly redressed and snuck back into the lounge to check if Rain was still asleep. But no, she's wide awake with the TV blasting. As I peek around the corner, she sits up and giggles.

"You know, if you're going to have phone sex with your boss, maybe disconnect your phone from the speaker next time."

I slap my hand over my mouth in horror.

"I'm so sorry!" It comes out muffled, but she just laughs.

"Don't worry, I shut it off as soon as I heard Chase's voice." She wags her finger playfully, giving me a mock scolding.

Grabbing her coat and slipping on her shoes, she pulls me into a quick hug.

"Have fun this weekend," she says with a wink. My cheeks burn as she throws me a cheeky smile over her shoulder before disappearing down the corridor, pushing her vintage bicycle down the steps. Despite her love for fast cars, Rain rides her bike everywhere she can. It's another reason why I love her. After Rain leaves my apartment I march over to my wardrobe, grab my silver dress and shove it inside my weekend bag.

•.................•.................•

I drag my legs downstairs and find Chase sitting in his car waiting for me at seven A.M. sharp in the car park. He flashes his headlights in my direction.

Hooking my bag over my shoulder, I take a deep breath and walk towards his BMW.

He pops open the boot and I place my cheap weekend bag right next to his Vuitton bag. I curl my hand around the cool metal handle and pull the door open to slip inside.

"Good morning, I got you a coffee".

I look down at the drinks holder to grab the steaming hot beverage. "Thank you".

I take a small sip and appreciate the creamy taste. He pulls out of the car park, and I shift my eyes to his strong hands gripping the steering wheel. At that moment I imagined what his hands would feel like around my neck, the muscles in his arms bulging as I screamed his name.

During the drive, Chase flips through his playlists, playing his favourite songs and singing along without a care. I sit back, half-listening, but mostly just watching him. There's something about the way he gets so into it—completely off-key at times, especially when he tries and fails to hit the high notes—that makes me laugh.

He catches my eye, grinning, and for a moment, it's just easy and fun between us. In an ideal world, a guy like him would pick a girl like me—just once, someone would make me their first choice. But I know better than to get caught up in that kind of fantasy. Still, sitting here, watching him, it's hard not to let my mind wander.

He asks about my childhood and how Rain and I became friends, and I find myself waving my hands animatedly as I recount the little details.

I catch him glancing away from the road, a warm smile spreading across his face.

My cheeks flush as I tuck my hair behind my ears, flustered, but I push on with my story. Chase keeps the conversation flowing, sharing tales about his parents and their move to Verona. Then, with a casual confidence, he adds, "You'd love Verona in winter."

My skin tingles at his words. *He thinks about what I'd love?* He's just flirting, Monica, I remind myself, trying to shake off the butterflies in my stomach. The rest of the drive is quiet, but there's this tension in the air. Every time he rests his hand on the console, I can't help but feel a little itch, wishing he'd just reach over and touch me. We don't bring up what happened last night. Which I'm glad about, after a short period of self-reflection last night I told myself that under no circumstances should that happen again. I failed miserably as I went to bed dreaming that it was Chase running his hands all over my body instead of mine.

•·················•·················•

We reach London within a few hours and pull up to the grand looking hotel where we'll be staying. Chase's car screeches against the tarmac as we pull into the underground car park. He exits the car and grabs our bags from the boot. I step out of the car and reach out to grab my bag from his hands, but he pulls away.

"Such a gentleman" I say as I brush past him. He walks up beside me after taking a few seconds to catch up.

"It takes a true gentleman to appreciate a view".

I whip my head around to face him and give him a light playful slap on his arm with my hand.

We walk up a short flight of stairs and reach the reception desk. Chase gives me a playful wink as he tells the receptionist our names. I lean against the cool marble desk, glancing around. The place has a sleek vibe—a restaurant and bar in the corner, and a small meeting room just next to it. It all reminds me of his hotel in Rome. The same kind of understated luxury. The memory tugs at me, bringing back the heat of that night. That I'm once again in a hotel with Chase.

"We're sorry sir, but it says right here that you requested one room".

My eyes pop out so hard they almost fall out of my head. I turn to face him and cross my arms.

"I swear I booked two rooms Monica".

I continue to stare at him, watching the lie slip out from his mouth.

"We got a call from a guy who said his name was Mr. Marino. He requested the change and confirmed all the details.", the blonde woman looked up and then continued to tap away on her computer.

"Okay, are there any spare rooms available tonight?" I ask, trying to take some control over the situation. She shakes her head.

"Sorry, we're fully booked".

My shoulders fall and butterflies flutter in my stomach. Avoiding him in the office has been nothing but hard work, but sharing a room with him? *This is not going to end well.*

Chase simply nods, signs the paperwork that she slides across the desk and grabs the white plastic keycard from her hands.

"I'm going to kill Jordan," Chase spits out as we make our way towards the lift. I admit defeat of the situation and decide to make light of it.

"You're sleeping in the bathtub, you know" I tell him as we step inside the lift. I lean back against the metal handrail as he drops our bags onto the floor. The metal doors slam shut behind him.

16 CHASE

I'm going to kill Jordan.

After, I thank him for his interference. I didn't think telling him where we were staying was going to backfire on me, but I didn't think he'd go this far. *Fair play to him, he wins this round.* I drop our bags to my feet with a satisfying thud as the lift doors close behind me. Monica watches me cautiously.

"If that's what you want" I give her a shrug and place my hands in my pocket. At this point I think I'd sleep in a bin if she asked me to. The lift pings on our floor. She nods her head. I bend down to grab the bags as she steps out onto the cream-coloured carpet.

I let her walk ahead and tell her, "Room 1822". She slows as she stops outside the wooden door of our room, and I pass her a keycard.

She pushes the door open, and we both walk in. We both freeze and stare at the queen-sized bed. Being alone in a hotel room with Monica again is going to be dangerous. I walk over to the desk and place our bags next to the complimentary bottle of champagne that is laying in a bucket of ice. I watch her as she takes slow steps around the room and then towards the bathroom. Images of us in the shower together cross my mind. The soapy water running down her body and off her tits. I imagine my thumb running over her bottom lip as I fuck her in the shower until she screams my name and begs me for more. She clears her throat causing me to snap out of my sex daydream. I shuffle over to unpack my clothes for this evening. She joins me by my side and copies my action with her own bag.

My heart skips a beat as she pulls out that sparkly silver dress that she wore that night in Rome. Jealousy invades every part of my body.

"You can't wear that" her head slowly turns as she looks at me with rage.

"Excuse me?" She places her hand on her chest.

I lower my voice, "Our client won't be looking at the contract, his attention will be elsewhere". *Like your fucking tits.*

We both turn, her body inches away from mine. I feel like a bull in a China shop around Monica. Her breathing picks up speed and her reaction causes my cock to strain against the fabric of my boxers. Her cheeks go warm and her eyes sparkle as she glares up at me.

"Mr Marino" she begins, "Do you have a problem with men looking at my body?".

Rage has now taken over every inch of my body. It's almost killed me not seeing her these past few weeks. The odd email she sent me, and video call wasn't enough. Especially after last night. So, I grab her ponytail and give it a light pull which causes her to bend her knees.

"Yes, I fucking do".

I quickly shoved our clothes and bags off the desk, letting her silver dress land on the bed. With one swift motion, I wrapped her legs around me and slammed her down onto the now-cleared desk. Leaning in, I growled, "It's mine."

Desperate for a taste, I pressed my lips to hers, and she opened her mouth, welcoming me in. Her small hands tangled in my hair, then slid down to my shoulders.

I ran my hands over her soft skin, feeling my rough fingers catch on her silky black shirt. Unable to hold back, I tore it open, buttons scattering like confetti. The gasp she let out made my pulse quicken. I snake my eyes over her body how's she's wearing a *red* fucking lace bra. I take a second to appreciate the sight before me. She's like a tainted goddess. Her slightly swollen lips smudged red lipstick, her rising chest and messy hair. "Fucking perfect."

I tell her as she leans back a little, like she already knows what I'm telling her.

Her fingers tug at the fabric of my shirt, "this needs to go".

My chest rumbles with a small laugh and I allow her to unbutton this very inconvenient barrier that's separating my skin from hers.

I hook my hands behind her to grip her ass and bring her towards me. Our tongues flick against each other as I reach for the bottom of her skirt. I wait for a couple of seconds, but she doesn't stop me. She jumps as I brush my thumb against the wetness of her underwear.

"You're soaking for me, Cherry". I slowly make my way down from her lips to her collarbones. The taste of her perfume appears on my tongue. Using my fingers I pull her underwear to the side and part her folds to dip two fingers in. Her head tips back and eyes roll slightly back into her skull. She lets out a moan as I use my thumb to apply firm pressure to her clit. The sound of her wetness causes a moan to escape from my own mouth. I continue until she grabs my wrist, and I stop.

She leans forward to unbuckle the belt of my trousers. I stare down to face her, my nose brushing against hers. Her head bobs a small nod.

"I want to", with her consent I pull off my belt and remove my trousers and kick them across the room, as she leans back on the desk to remove her skirt and underwear.

"I'm clean," I tell her. I immediately got checked after that night at the pub with that girl who I'm sure would've passed something onto me.

"Me too and I'm on the pill", she breathes out.

Monica reaches out and hooks her fingers into the waistband of my boxers.

I tut my teeth at her, "So eager Cherry".

"Shut up and fuck me Chase".

I don't waste any time. I pull down my boxers and watch as my cock springs free. Her eyes go wide at the sight of me, which gives my ego a good stroke. I grip my rock-hard cock, pump a few times and place the head at her slick wet entrance. We fit fucking perfectly, like she was made for me. She inhales sharply as I slowly push my way inside of her and we both let out a moan in unison.

I decided right then that Monica is my something *more.*

17 MONICA

The sight of Chase slowly pulling out and then slamming into me again, drives my release to the surface. My thighs tremble as one of his hands grips me and the other hand is placed firmly around my neck. Every sensation is heightened. I can even feel the pulse in my neck against the rough skin of his hands.

My imagination from this morning of his hands around my neck does not do justice to how it actually feels. My mouth goes dry from the rapid breaths escaping my body.

Chase removes the hand that grips my thigh and begins to circle my clit.

"You like that?" I nod my head slowly.

"Come for me, like the good girl that you are", my body reacts to his command and the pressure causes me to jolt forward as my high hits.

His name bursts from my lips and his movements become faster and faster. My fingernails dig in and grip the back of his neck as he chases his own release. He lets out a deep groan as he drops his head to my shoulder.

Stars dance across my vision as Chase brings his head from my shoulder to rest his forehead against mine.

"Fucking perfect" he repeats his words from earlier. He grips my sides as slowly slips out of me. I watch him slip into the bathroom, the sound of the shower turning on echoing softly through the room. A minute later, Chase emerges, clad in a plush white robe stitched with the hotel's logo on the left breast. He holds another robe in his hands, a playful smile tugging at the corners of his mouth. Without a word, he strides over to me, draping the robe around my shoulders and guiding my arms into the sleeves, his touch warm and inviting. He removes his hands from me, and I already miss his touch.

"Chase, that was amazing, but we probably shouldn't do that again" I told him as I slid off the desk, tying up my robe. He moves to stand beside me, popping the champagne that was waiting for us in the room, "Whatever you want Cherry".

I give him a coy smirk and watch the bubbles float to the top as he fills a glass and hands it to me. The ice-cold liquid cools my dry throat.

"Ahhh, that's so good". He gazes at me from over the rim of his glass, a smile playing on his lips.

After taking a sip, he sets his champagne down on the desk and strides quickly to his bag, checking the screen of his phone.

Chase runs his fingers through his hair and chuckles, "Fuck. We're going to be late".

I almost completely forgot the whole purpose of this trip.

Springing into action I place my own glass onto the wooden desk. My hands fumble with the belt of my robe as I turn my back to him and stroll towards the bathroom.

"I can be ready in thirty minutes; let me just grab a quick shower first."

The floor becomes distant as he swoops me up, tosses me effortlessly over his shoulder as if I weigh nothing at all.

"But showering together will be so much quicker," he teases, his voice low and playful. The playful slap of his hand on my ass sends a giggle bubbling up from my lips.

The steam from the shower surrounds me as I stare down at Chase, who currently has his head between my legs.

"How is this quick… - *Oh god*", my question is cut short as Chase sucks hard on my clit.

My hand flies to the wall beside me to steady myself. His hands tightly grip my ass as he devours me.

"But you taste so good" he brings his head back to look up and tell me. His tongue laps at me over and over. I begin to question him again, but my climax interrupts me. He stands to give me a kiss and I can taste myself on his lips.

I turn to face the shower as Chase stands behind me, his cock digging into my upper back, and watch his hands as he lathers soap onto my tits and stomach. We wash and turn off the shower. Chases hooks a tie around his neck as I slip into my silver dress. He lets out a deep groan as I slip on my matching silver heels. *I know how much it's killing him - and I fucking love it.*

My heels click in time with Chase's footsteps as we make our way across the hotel reception floor toward the restaurant, where our client and their team are waiting for us. Chase, ever the gentleman, opens the glass door for me—then cheekily pinches my ass as I walk through. I throw a squinted glare over my shoulder, but a small smirk creeps onto my face. As we approach the table, a man with silver hair waves us over, and I pull myself back into a professional mode.

We exchanged introductions and ordered drinks for the table, and as I settled into my seat across from the client and his team, I could feel the excitement crackling in the air. Chase leaned in, exuding confidence like a warm glow.

I couldn't help but steal glances at him; his smoothness in engaging with the clients was impressive, and his perfectly timed jokes had everyone laughing. When our eyes met, a rush of excitement coursed through me, warming my cheeks. Every time his hand brushed against my thigh under the table, it felt like fire igniting my skin.

Each time I flicked his hand away, he'd just grip mine, seamlessly continuing the conversation across the table.

I tried to shake off the distraction, reminding myself I was here to do a job. Not stare at Chase's gorgeously structured face.

But with the sexual chemistry between us, it was hard to focus on anything else in the room.

I take charge of the second half of the meeting, feeling the pleasant buzz from a good meal and a couple of drinks. Standing up, I confidently walk through my proposal, earning nods and smiles from the team. The energy around the table lifts me, and as I finish, I give a small, playful bow, which draws a round of chuckles from the table. The team takes their time signing the contract, but once it's sealed, they stand to thank us for the evening.

Chase and I shake hands with our newly secured client, walking them out of the hotel with a sense of accomplishment. With the signed contract in hand, we head back inside.

My arm brushes against Chase's as we ride up in the lift, the soft hum of the elevator filling the silence. He turns, placing one hand against the wall behind me, leaning slightly as he gazes into the mirror.

"You did a great job today, Monica. You should be proud of yourself," he says, his voice low and warm. Butterflies swirl in my chest and stomach. I shift to face him, and he mirrors the movement, his intense gaze locking onto mine. For a moment, I can't tear my eyes away from the man who's given me so much confidence in such a short time. I glance down, nervously playing with the bracelet on my wrist.

"Thank you," I murmur, feeling a quiet sense of pride. "I felt good."

"Next time you can lead the whole meeting. I'm confident you'll do great but for now let's head upstairs and order some room service"

He closes the space between us and slowly moves my hair to the side.

"I'd like that" I whisper. The lift pings and we step out and walk towards our room.

Our room. Fuck.

There's a certain thrill in doing something I know I shouldn't, and it feels exhilarating. If this is the start of something between us, I can already sense that I'll be the one left picking up the pieces. Men like Chase are notorious for breaking hearts, and I've had my share of heartache to know better. But that night we first met, when he brushed the lipstick off my cheek, something ignited between us - a tiny spark I can't ignore. I deserve to be happy, and who am I to stand in the way of my own happiness?

My legs come to a halt at the door as I turn to Chase, noticing his eyes widen in surprise. He places his warm hand on my arm and asks, "Everything okay?"

I nod. "Yes, but if we're going to do this, we need some rules."

He shifts his feet and crosses his arms, a smirk etched on his face. "For dinner?"

A giggle escapes me as I quickly cover my mouth and swat at his chest. "No, I mean us. Me and you." Chase looks at me like a kid in a candy store, excitement flickering in his gaze.

"Okay, let's talk." He swipes the keycard and pushes the door open but stops to turn back to me with a playful smirk.

"But I'm not sleeping in the bathtub."

I roll my eyes and follow him inside, a smile tugging at my lips.

18 CHASE

The steady patter of rain against the hotel window jolts me awake, the soft sound filling the room. I glance outside at the grey, wet morning before looking down at Monica, her legs draped over mine. My hands glide over her smooth, bronzed skin as she stirs slightly. This morning is unfolding the way the night we first met should have—with our legs tangled in the sheets, her head resting against my chest. I stroke her hair as she looks up at me with sleepy eyes.

"Good morning, Cherry," I say quietly. A playful smirk tugs at her lips.

"Good morning Chase" she says trying to stifle a yawn. I brush a stray hair from her cheek and meet her gaze. She nestles her head onto my chest, the rain still tapping rhythmically against the glass.

The sheets feel cold as Monica slips out and makes slow steps towards the coffee machine. She's wearing my shirt which she makes look like a dress.

"Double espresso?" she turns her head and asks, which causes me to sit up.

"Yeah? How'd you know?".

"You're my boss, it's kind of important that I remember how you have your coffee", then she turns her back to me and begins humming. I fall back to my pillow, in absolute awe. Last night, Monica laid down some ground rules. 'No sex in the office, no sending nudes over email and no teasing touches under the table during meetings. Agreeing to her rules, I placed my hand on my chest, stuck one hand down my boxers and repeated her words back to her. She could barely finish her sentence without laughing but if she needs rules then I'll happily abide. Monica skips over to me and hands me my coffee. My heart begins to race, and I don't think it's from the caffeine. I set my empty coffee cup onto the bedside table and stand to place myself behind Monia. I snake my hands around her waist and watch her as she effortlessly repacks her bag.

We stayed up most of the night talking the conversation effortlessly flowing between us. She sat opposite me on the bed, legs crossed, watching my lips move as I spoke. I told her about the Australia expansion I'm planning, how I'm thinking of buying more property in Manchester, and the award show happening in Paris this November. At the mention of the city, her eyes lit up, sparkling with excitement.

"Oh, we should definitely go ice skating on the Eiffel Tower," she said with a grin. I chuckled and quickly reminded her that the team would be there too.

"They can come ice skating as well," she replied with a playful smirk. "I'm sure they won't notice if we sneak off for a few minutes."

The thought of sneaking around with her is torture, not being able to show the world that she's mine—but it will make Monica happy plus the sight of her on her knees, my cock in her mouth? Pure bliss.

"But doesn't that go against the rules?" I teased, raising an eyebrow. She rolled her eyes, lips twitching into a smile.

"We won't be in the office." I slapped her ass for her sassiness and then proceeded to shove my cock hard inside her again as punishment.

My car grumbles as we begin our journey to leave London behind and head back to Manchester and Monica takes control of the music this time. I must admit her style in music shocked me. Her playlist is heavier than mine and it causes the bass to buzz through the speakers of my BMW. It's not what I expected from her, but it suits her—bold, unapologetic, unique. Her leg bounces nervously against the footwell, her hands fidgeting as if she's wrestling with something unspoken. I glance over at her, feeling the tension radiating from her. Without a word, I reach over and place my hand on her bouncing leg. The moment my hand touches her, the movement stills.

"Everything okay, sweetheart?" My voice is soft, but the concern is clear.

She hesitates for a second, then whispers, "Jane doesn't seem to like me very much."

Jane? That catches me off guard. I wasn't expecting her to bring her up, but I can see how it's been eating at her. I try to reassure her, though I'm not sure how well I'll manage.

"Jane doesn't like anyone. She's just jealous of you." Monica turns her head towards me, curiosity and uncertainty in her eyes.

"What do you mean?"

I clear my throat, keeping my gaze fixed on the road.

"There was... a moment between us last year. At the Christmas party. But it didn't go beyond a kiss, and I'm not interested in her."

The words hang heavy in the air, and I can feel her shifting uncomfortably in her seat. The silence that follows is deafening. I know I've messed up. *Nice job, Chase.*

Not even twenty-four hours in and I've already managed to screw things up. My grip tightens on the steering wheel, and I glance at her from the corner of my eye, wishing I could take back the tension I've just thrown between us.

•·················•·················•

We drove back to Manchester in complete silence. The only words I get from her is when she thanks me when I drop her back to her apartment. Sitting in the car park of her apartment I contemplate following her inside, but she clearly needs space.

So instead of barging upstairs like a caveman, I grab my phone that's sitting in the centre console and find a local florist.

My fingers tap against the screen as I type the address into the navigation of my car and head in the direction of the florist. Pulling up to an empty space outside the shop, I drag my sorry ass inside and order a dozen red roses to Monica's apartment.

"Thank you, and what is the delivery address sir?" the young girl asks me from behind the counter as she grabs a small white slip of paper and pulls out the payment machine. As I hand her my credit card, I can't help but notice how young she is, how full of life she is, how her father would hate for anyone to break her little heart. I can't bear the thought of upsetting Monica. I couldn't do that to Carlos either.

"I'll deliver these myself actually, thank you".

The thorns from the roses dig deep into my hands as I open my car door and carefully place them onto the passenger seat. I cruise down the high street back to Monica's apartment, pull into her car park, turn off the engine and head to her door. Roses digging into my head, I squint at the names on the list and find her last name next to her apartment number. The intercom buzzes as I wait for her to voice to pipe down the speaker. My feet bounce as I eagerly wait for her to answer. I tap the buzzer again.

"Hello?" She sings.

I clear my throat, "Hi, it's Chase". *Please let me in.*

The lock on the door clicks, "Door's open".

I sprint up the stairs and stop on her floor. I round the corner of the corridor and find her leaning against the door. She's dressed in tight grey joggers, a black hoodie with a band logo on and pink fluffy socks - and she's never looked so god damn sexy.

She beckons me with a casual wave, and I step inside, following her into the heart of her apartment. My eyes take in the space, a reflection of her vibrant personality. The aqua blue sofa sits invitingly before a sleek flat screen TV, while a wooden coffee table, centred in the room, holds a tray of candles, their soft scent subtly perfuming the air. Bright, colourful paintings in a lively Spanish style adorn the walls, filling the space with warmth and character. She moves forward gracefully, and I, hiding the roses behind my back, slowly bring them forward. Her eyes shift to the green and deep red bouquet. She lets out a small giggle.

"Thank you for the flowers, you didn't need to". Suddenly, I'm the one feeling nervous, I try to lighten the tension.

"Actually, they're for me", I give her a coy smirk. She lights slaps my hand and grabs the flowers from me as I pull her into a hug.

"I'm sorry. I probably shouldn't have told you that about Jane. First thing Monday morning, I'm firing her". She shakes her head against my arm as she pulls away.

"I don't want you to do that. I just have to get used to the fact that your list of…erm…past lovers might be a little longer than mine". Now, it's me that giggles.

"She's definitely not a past lover and my list isn't that long, thank you very much". Monica moves towards the kitchen, cradling the bouquet of roses I gave her. As she turns on the tap to fill a vase, I can't help but wonder about her past. How many people have been lucky enough to know her like this? The thought makes me uneasy.

"So, have you had many... erm... past lovers?" I ask, leaning casually against the counter, though I feel anything but casual inside. My eyes follow her movements as she fills the glass vase, her back turned to me. When she turns to face me, her cheeks are flush pink and there's a hint of shyness in her eyes.

"Erm, if you count two as a long list," she says, with a small, nervous smile. Two? My chest tightens, and my palms suddenly feel clammy. As she opens a drawer and pulls out a pair of kitchen scissors to trim the stems, I clear my throat, trying to steady my voice.

"How old are you?".

A crease forms on her brow, confusion washing over her face.

"I just turned twenty-four. Why?"

I tap my foot against the wooden floor, tension creeping up my spine.

"Please tell me I'm in addition to those two." She places the scissors onto the kitchen counter and takes a step closer to me, a playful glint in her eyes.

"Yes, why?"

The relief is immediate, but it doesn't stop the nervous energy coursing through me.

"Don't you want to be with someone closer to your age?" The words come out sharper than I intended, but it's the nerves speaking, not me.

She wrinkles her nose, looking almost disgusted.

"Chase, I want to be with you. I'm done with silly boys. I need a man."

She twirls a finger around a loose strand of her hair, and something stirs deep in my chest—a flutter I wasn't expecting. I smile, the tension between us easing.

"Alright then, a man you shall have," I say, wrapping my arm around her waist and pulling her closer. I bend down and press my lips to hers, soft and slow, savouring the moment. She tugs at the collar of my shirt, and just like that, my body reacts, desire heating my blood. But then, with a teasing smile, she steps back, her hands falling to her sides.

"See you on Monday, Mr Marino," she says, her voice laced with playful mischief.

I take a step back, smiling at the girl who's got me wrapped around her finger. She walks me to the door, watching as I head down the corridor before closing it behind me. And as I walk away, I can't help but smile. This woman, she's already turning my world upside down.

But I currently have one thought at this moment in time. *I need a fucking drink.* As my shoes click against the staircase of her apartment, I pull out my phone and call Jordan. But he doesn't answer. I flick through my contacts and find Noah's number. Thankfully he answers straight away.

"Hey boss, what's up?", his voice shouts over chatter and conversation in the background of the call. "Hey, have you seen Jordan?" I push open the main door and walk around the building to my car. "Yep, he's right next to me." Noah replies.

"Tell him to answer his fucking phone, where are you guys?" I slip into my car and wait for his response.

"Dog and Gun. Are you coming down for a drink?" Noah questions.

"Already on my way" I end the call and slip my phone into my pocket. Within a few minutes I pull into the car park of the pub and enter inside to find Jordan and Noah sitting in the corner, where there's an ice-cold glass of whiskey waiting for me.

"Ahhh, I needed that." I sigh in relief as the cool liquid slides down my throat, instantly calming the tension in my shoulders.

"Did you just get back from London?" Jordan asks as he deals out the playing cards, his voice casual. I lean back against the wooden booth and hum in response, nodding slightly.

"How was Monica's performance?" The sound of her name jolts me, and my neck cracks with how fast I snap my head up, staring at Noah. His brow furrowed in confusion, beer in hand.

"Her proposal performance?" he clarifies, lifting the bottle to his lips. My heart slows its frantic pace. I exhale, relieved.

"Oh, yeah. It was fine. She was great, handled it like a pro. She's a great asset to the company." Jordan sniggers across the table. I try to sound nonchalant, but inside I'm a mess. I haven't even made it to the office yet, and I'm already paranoid. I couldn't care less who knows about me and Monica, but she wants to keep things under wraps. And for her, I'll play along. As the night wears on, we order food and a few more rounds of beer.

The pub is dim, the low hum of chatter creating a comfortable background noise. I take the cards from Jordan and begin shuffling them, getting ready for the next round. The door to the pub creaks open, but I stay focused on the cards in my hands.

"Hey Chase, isn't that Monica and Rain? But who's the blonde girl?" Jordan's voice cuts through my concentration. I shift my gaze from the cards to him, then to the door. Noah places his beer down, eyes wide.

"Wow, she's gorgeous," he murmurs, clearly impressed. It takes my eyes a few seconds to focus, and I realise that I know the blonde that Noah is making puppy dog eyes at.

Skye, my interior designer walks in behind Monica and Rain. I didn't know they all knew each other? But the world really is a small place sometimes.

My eyes follow theirs, landing on Monica and her friends as they walk in, arms linked and laughing together. The sight of her immediately tugs a smile to my lips. Monica looks radiant, so carefree. She's magnetic, effortlessly drawing all eyes to her. But it's not just the way she looks. It's the way she makes me feel—like I'm the only one who really sees her. And even though we're keeping things quiet for now, seeing her here, so close yet just out of reach, stirs something possessive inside me.

"The blonde girl is Skye"

I inform

Jordan whips his head towards me.

"Wait. That's Rain's sister?"

"How do you know Rain and Skye are related?" Jordan shrugs at me before responding.

“She told me in Rome”

Oh.

“Wait, you guys met Rain and Monica in Rome?” Now it’s Noah’s turn to furrow his eyebrows at us as he questions.

I have some explaining to do.

19 MONICA

Watching Chase stroll down the corridor, I smile at the man who thinks about me enough to buy me flowers when I'm upset. No one has ever brought me flowers (apart from my dad), but this is exactly why I'm done with boys and need a man. No guy has ever made me orgasm more than once during a relationship let alone in a single night. Chase immediately notices when something is bugging me or has me down. But hearing Chase admit that something happened between him and Jane stung. My heart rested a little when he told me it was just a kiss. From the way Jane acted around me I thought something more happened at some point. Nonetheless, I won't let Jane get to me anymore. I won't allow her to pick on me, like a bully. And I easily recognise bullies.

When I was younger, my mother always pointed out things she knew I was insecure about. How I was a little taller than most of the girls my age. How I had put on some weight during my early teen years. And especially how my teeth used to stick out a little at the front. She constantly reminded me to cover my hideous teeth with my hand whenever I laughed. Even though my teeth had straightened out now, *thank God for braces,* I still carried the last piece of toxicity from her with me every day.

I brushed past the roses from Chase sitting on my kitchen counter, their sweet scent lingering as I made my way to my bedroom. I flopped face down onto my bed, sinking into the comfort of the mattress like it was calling my name. Just then, my phone buzzed in my pocket, pulling me back to reality. I pulled it out and saw Rain's name pop up on the screen.

With a roll of my eyes, I tapped the accept button.

"Nope, I'm already in my comfy clothes!" I groaned into the phone. I could already picture Rain shaking her head at me, probably ready to convince me to change out of my sweats. But honestly, right now, all I wanted was to sink into my cosy cocoon and forget about the world.

"But it's Saturday" Rain whines. "You can't stay in on a Saturday night plus I owe you a night out." Another groan escapes me. "Skye could really do with a night out too".

She really knows how to guilt trip me.

"Fine, give me an hour and I'll meet you at dads". I pull the phone away from my ear as she squeals down the speaker. Ending the call, I pull myself off the bed and drag myself into the shower.

As the soap bubbles over my legs, I notice small bruises from my night in the hotel with Chase. A smile tugs my lips as I remember his hands all over me. My body felt loose and relaxed with him, his strong hands would grip me so hard, sending jolts of lightning every time he touched me. I'm stuck in this whirlwind of thoughts, flashing back to the night before. Seriously, how could one guy be so incredibly perfect and yet make my heart race with anxiety? He was an absolute god of a man, with that killer smile and charm that could light up the whole room. I mean, I was totally swept up in the moment, laughing and joking with him, but now I couldn't help but think about the heartbreak lurking just around the corner. I knew this crush was bound to lead me to some serious pain—way worse than the little bruises I had. I could still picture his hand brushing against mine and the warmth in his eyes that made everything feel electric. But with every sweet moment we shared, I felt the weight of what would eventually come crashing down. One day, all of this would shatter, leaving me with nothing but memories and that familiar ache in my chest. I loved those moments, but I couldn't shake the feeling that it was all just setting me up for a fall. Now I was upsetting myself with all my thinking. I switched the shower off and decided to stop being so miserable and pessimistic. Wrapping the soft towel around myself, my red speaker chimes as I connect my phone and play a song that Chase had shown me on the drive to London yesterday morning. I throw my phone down on the bed and dance on my feet a little as I stand in front of my full-length mirror, taking a second to appreciate my reflection and the smile across my face and begin to apply my mascara. As the wand pushes my eyelashes up, the lyrics 'If I can't have you, nobody can' float across the room from the speaker. Why didn't I pick up on those words yesterday? I take a step back, turn and kneel onto my bed. Caught up in the music, I grab my phone and snap a full nude photo of myself in the mirror and send it to Chase along with a playful message.

I slip into my silver dress, matching heels and grab my white leather jacket. The sound of my heels taps in the stairwell of my apartment as I make my way downstairs to wait for a taxi. A breeze of wind brushes across my face and neck, causing goosebumps to appear across my skin. *I wish I was still wearing my comfy clothes.* I bounce on my feet a little to keep myself warm. It's now early evening and the sun is beginning to set, shades of pink and purple ignite the sky across Manchester. My taxi pulls up and I step inside, my teeth still chattering a little from the cold. We cruise down the high street and the same song from earlier plays on the radio inside the taxi. The words 'If I can't have you, nobody can' once again sit in my head. That causes me to look down at the reply I got from Chase.

Me:

All yours

Mr Marino:

You kill me Cherry...

I already can't wait to see him on Monday. I know I set rules for us when we're in the office, but I won't lie—it's going to be difficult keeping my hands off him. I'll just have to settle for daydreaming instead.

Pushing thoughts of next week aside, I step out of the taxi and thank the driver. Rain and Skye are already outside the pub, arms waving wildly in the air to get my attention. I smile and wave back, making my way towards them.

But as I do, something catches my eye. The café across the road still has its lights on. At nearly nine pm? I pause, my gaze drawn to three shadowy figures leaning against the window. A strange feeling creeps over me as I watch them. One of the figures turns abruptly and pulls the blinds shut. A chill runs down my spine just as Cathay, the café owner, walks to the door and flips the sign from 'Open' to 'Closed.' I shake it off and decide to mind my own business, making a mental note to ask dad how much he knows about this woman.

Rain squeals with excitement as we hug, loop our arms, and head inside. It's busy for a Saturday night, but we find a free table on the right side of the bar. My dad brings over a bottle of rosé and three glasses before heading back to the bar, but Skye stands up to follow him.

"One second, girls, just need to ask Carlos something," she says, patting Rain's shoulder before walking off. I glance at Rain, raising an eyebrow as I open the bottle.

"What was that about?" I ask, passing her a glass.

She rolls her eyes. "I have no idea." She takes a big gulp, nearly draining half the glass in one sip.

"Okay, strange," I say, laughing lightly. "Anyway, how's work?"

I lean back in my wooden seat, waiting for her reply. She chats excitedly about how well things are going, mentioning that, like me, her boss has entrusted her with major accounts and high-profile clients. Then she grins, eyes lighting up. "Oh, and I adopted the cutest little black kitten. Her name's Luna."

"Aww, I've got to come over and meet your new baby," I say with a smile.

"She's absolutely adorable!" Rain gushes. Just then, I spot Skye returning from the bar, a heavy sigh escaping her as she drops into the chair.

"Everything alright?" I ask, pouring a glass of wine and sliding it towards her.

"Yes, all good now. So, what are we talking about?" Skye asks as she brings the glass to her lips, the pink gloss from her lips sticks to the rim.

"Monica was just telling me how she fucked her boss in London". Wine squirts out through my nose as Rain reaches over to hand me a napkin.

"Oh my god, Rain." I glance at Skye. "I wasn't," I said quickly. She raises an eyebrow, but a soft giggle escapes her.

"Good, because you know how messy things can get if you ever start something with your boss."

That familiar sinking feeling washes over me, the kind where you wish the ground would just open and swallow you whole. Skye keeps going, oblivious.

"Trust me, I know from experience. Mixing business with pleasure rarely leads to a fairytale ending."

Maybe she's right. Maybe she's wrong. *God, I hope she's wrong.*

I glance at the empty wine bottle and stand to grab another.

"Can you get a red this time? I can pretend it's Steve's blood then," Skye mutters, her voice dripping with sarcasm. I catch it, even though she tries to say it under her breath. I really hope she finds someone who'll appreciate her the way she deserves.

"Red, please, Dad," I say as I lean over the slightly sticky wooden bar, resting my head in my hands, feeling the weight of everything pressing down on me. My dad's familiar, warm voice pulls me out of my thoughts.

"¿Qué te pasa, mi amor?" His Spanish accent, thick and comforting, wraps around the words like a hug. He walks back with the bottle of red in hand—Skye's "blood" request fulfilled.

"I'm okay, Dad. Just… a little stressed," I lift my head and force a smile, hoping it hides the turmoil inside. He shakes his head with a gentle sigh.

"You're too young to be stressed. Go, have fun, mija."

The tenderness in his voice, mixed with that accent I've known my whole life, makes my chest tighten. He's right. No point in stressing over something I can't control.

I smile softly, take the bottle from him, and walk back to the table, feeling just a little lighter.

The three of us laugh and catch up on high school gossip, who's doing what and who's doing who.

"Nature calls. I won't be a second," I say, slipping away from the table to find the bathroom. The alcohol buzz has my vision a bit fuzzy, so I tread carefully. After I've finished, I step out of the cubicle to wash my hands, catching my reflection in the mirror.

With a quick swipe, I pull out my ruby-red lipstick and reapply, watching as my lips plump up. Feeling bold, I grab my phone from my purse, snap a selfie, and hit send to Chase.

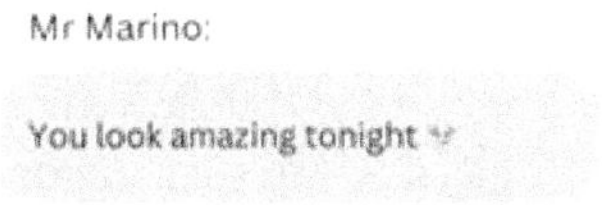

I step out of the bathroom, still riding the confidence high from my lipstick touch-up, and nearly collide with someone coming out of the men's room.

"Hello, have we met before?" The familiar scent and deep, chocolate-brown eyes tell me exactly who it is. Chase stands there, smirking down at me.

"Hey, what are you doing here?" I ask, trying to keep my surprise in check.

He shrugs, a playful glint in his eye. "Out with Noah and Jordan for a few drinks. Fancy joining us?" He takes a step closer, and suddenly, it's not just the space between us shrinking. The energy between us feels electric, humming in the air.

"Sure, let me check with the girls first," I say, spinning on my heels. But before I can take a step, Chase's hand finds my arm, and he pulls me in for a kiss, warm and lingering.

"I've wanted to do that since the second you walked in," he murmurs against my lips, sending a shiver down my spine. Standing on my tiptoes, I lean into him and kiss him back, feeling the world around us fade for a moment.

"We're sitting in the corner, near the jukebox," he says, finally letting me go, though his fingers trail down my arm as if reluctant to break the contact.

I return to our table, where Rain and her sister Skye are waiting. "So… Chase invited us to join him and his friends," I say casually, though I can't hide the spark in my eyes.

Skye narrows her gaze, her voice laced with caution. "Mon, is that a good idea?" She looks at me, clearly worried, but I shrug it off. I know her hearts in the right place, but tonight, maybe it's the wine but all I want is to let loose and have a bit of fun. "Yeah, come on. I'm sure everything will be fine". We grab the remaining bottle of wine, our glasses and make our way over to the guys. *The guys? Oh god.* One moment, I was buried in textbooks, spending every Saturday night cramming for exams, only emerging from my room for snack breaks and caffeine refills. And now, somehow, I'm here—feeling almost like an actual adult. If things had turned out differently, *she'd* be here too, watching me stumble my way through this new life: balancing a job, managing my own apartment, and navigating a relationship with my boyfriend… who just so happens to be her boss. But now is not the time for sad thoughts.

I clear my throat as we approach the table where Chase, Jordan, and Noah are sitting. When they spot us, they rise to greet us.

"Evening, ladies. Rain, how are you?" Chase asks, reaching out to shake her hand. Rain's gaze flickers briefly toward Jordan as she replies, "I've been great, thank you."

Chase gives a polite nod and turns to Skye, extending his hand with a smile. "And you must be Skye."

Skye takes a moment, watching us all with a raised brow. "Wait, have you all met before?"

This time, Jordan speaks up, flashing a grin. "It's a long story. Why don't you grab a seat, and I'll get us some drinks?"

We shuffle into place around the long table, taking our time as Jordan heads to the bar. I naturally slide into the seat next to Chase, while Rain sits across from me, leaving space beside her for Jordan. Skye settles at the end, facing Noah, who is seated to Chase's right.

I settle back into my seat, trying to relax, but my leg tenses as Chase's hand slides to my upper thigh, his grip firm and teasing. I swat his hand away, leaning over to whisper, "Behave yourself."

He grins, leaning in close enough for his breath to tickle my ear. "But we're not in the office," he murmurs, his voice laced with mischief.

20 CHASE

Jordan returns to the table with not one or two but three fucking bottles of wine. I shake my head at him. But he's the least of my concerns right now.

At this moment, Monica is sitting right next to me, bronze skin on show.

Tempting me like a piece of caramel, that I want to immediately put in between my teeth. I bring my hand back to her thigh and she gives in, allowing me to rest my hand there.

My cock tenses at the memory of how Monica's pussy tastes. I'm addicted, she's like a drug to me. I could devour her every night and I'd still go back for more. Craving her until she begs me to stop.

In my peripheral vision, I spot Skye eyeing us up. Monica told me about her, she's cautious and protective.

But I'm also protective. I wouldn't hurt Monica, and I'd kill anyone that does. I need to explain to Skye that we're on the same side. The conversation flows around the table, and whilst everyone's attention is elsewhere, I sneak Monica a quick kiss on her jaw. I whisper that I'll be back in a second. A shiver races down my spine as the cool evening air wraps around me. I step outside for a quick smoke—something I wouldn't usually do, but tonight, let's call it social smoking, even if I'm on my own. I flick my lighter, igniting the small vice between my fingers, and take a deep inhale, letting the smoke fill my lungs. Just as I exhale, a voice breaks through the night.

"Hey, Chase."

"Hey, Skye. How's it going?" I turn to face her, the warmth of the pub's chatter fading behind me. I try to break the awkward silence.

"Nice job you did a few weeks ago on those apartments over in Bowdon by the way".

"Thanks Chase".

She takes a deep breath in.

"Listen…" She tugs at the sleeves of her white leather jacket, a hint of tension radiating from her. I feel like a cat caught with a mouse, heart racing as I brace myself for what's coming next.

"I'm listening." She meets my gaze, her expression serious.

"Monica is like a sister to me, and I'm not blind. Whatever is happening between you two is none of my business, but I'll only say this once: do not hurt her."

A light drizzle begins to fall, chilling the air and raising goosebumps along my arms. I can feel the hairs on the back of my neck stand on end.

"I won't," I reply, my voice steady, though I can feel the weight of her words pressing down on me.

Skye gives me a tight smile before turning to head back inside the bustling pub. I exhale slowly, watching my breath mingle with the misty air, then toss my cigarette onto the pavement, where it dances for a moment before settling on the wet ground.

Monica's skin pebbles as I graze my hand across her arm, taking my seat next to her. Over the next hour each person from our little party leaves to go home. Jordan and Noah are the last to leave the table. Monica barks out a laugh watching Noah struggle to drag all 6'3" of my brother out of the door. One hand covers her mouth while the other slaps the table, her laughter bubbling over as she fights for breath. I turn to face her, curiosity getting the better of me.

"Why do you cover your mouth when you laugh?" I rest my hand on hers, noticing how her smile falters.

"My mother," she replies, her voice softer now. "She used to pick on me about my teeth."

"What? I'm so sorry, mia cara."

Her shoulders rise and fall in a shrug, a flicker of vulnerability crossing her face. "I'm over it now," she says, though there's a hint of sadness in her tone.

"I just can't seem to shake this toxic habit she taught me." My chest hurts suddenly.

"Okay, let me help you then. Every time I catch you doing that, I'll punish you." Monica's cheeks go fire red. The sound of Carlos ringing the last order's bell fills the pub and pulls us from our moment.

“I should get going,” Monica whispers as she puts her arms through the sleeves of her own white leather jacket. Monica, Rain and Skye all have the same one, each with their initials stitched on the left-hand side next to the zip.

“Stay with me tonight Cherry”. The words slip out as she stands. She eyes me suspiciously.

“I’ll even sleep in the bathtub if you want”. She giggles again, but this time her hand flinches.

She doesn’t cover her mouth this time. Thank God because her smile is beautiful.

Monica nods her head. I grab her hand and drag her outside to wait for a taxi. The city lights blur as I stare out of the window, leaning my chin on Moncia resting her head on my chest. The streetlights feel brighter tonight.

I loop Monica’s arm around my shoulder, balancing her weight as I fumble with the door to my apartment with my other hand.

The lock clicks open, and as we step inside, the sensor lights flicker on, casting a warm glow over the space. Monica lifts her heavy head to take in her surroundings, her eyes widening in awe as they dance over my furniture, the sleek TV, the marble kitchen, and the vibrant art adorning the walls. “Wow,” she breathes, clearly impressed.

With a gentle nudge, I guide her to lean against the kitchen island, her gaze still wandering. I dash into my bedroom, grabbing one of my T-shirts for her, then head to the kitchen to fill a glass with water.

I quickly grab a soft dressing gown from the bathroom before returning to her side, ready to help her unwind. Her small hands fly up as I unzip her dress and pull my grey Nike t-shirt over her head and wrap the dressing gown around her small body. I bend down to unstrap her shoes and throw them to the side. Her hand flies to her mouth as she yawns. Monica, dressed in my clothes, in my kitchen, in my space. She looks nothing short of perfect.

I take her through to my bedroom and place her carefully on the sheets, her eyelids go heavy as I pull the covers up to her chin.

“Stay with me Chase”. I kiss her forehead and swing round the bed to join her. Throwing my arm around the back of my head, Monica turns to lean on my chest.

“Good night, Cherry”.

After a few minutes, her breathing slows, and I can tell she’s drifted off. Careful not to disturb her, I slip my shirt off, moving slowly so I don’t wake her. I toss it across the room, then quietly work my trousers off, one careful movement at a time. I won’t sleep naked, but I just want to feel closer to her, to feel her warmth against me. I settle in, wrapping her gently in my arms, and finally let myself relax. With Monica fast asleep on me, everything feels right.

21 MONICA

Imagine construction workers drilling, someone repeatedly hitting wooden planks with a hammer and the thumping bass of a very loud nightclub. All of those sounds together equal how hard my head is throbbing right now. I groan escapes me as I open my eyelids, one by one. It takes me a few seconds to realise, this is not my apartment.

"Good morning" I turn and find myself face to face with my boss.

"Good morning, Mr Marino".

He nuzzles my nose before placing a soft kiss on my lips.

"Do you have any painkillers? My head is killing me". He reaches behind him and produces a small box. I slowly sit up to grab the glass of water next to me. Chase watches as my throat bobs, swallowing the painkillers and water.

“Thank you”, I tell him as my heavy head falls back to my pillow. “For last night too. Looking after me.”

“Anything for you Cherry” he lifts the sheets from atop his muscled tattooed body and moves to stand at the edge of the bed. I have the perfect view of his entire body, including the bulge in his boxers. *Hello morning wood.*

My mind starts to wonder, and I clear my throat.

“Do you mind if I grab a shower?” I ask him, feeling the need to wash away the lingering smell of alcohol.

“Only if you don’t mind me joining you,” he replies with a playful smirk.

Well, I’m not going to say no.

I swing my legs over the side of the bed and let him lead me to his enormous bathroom. The counter is a dazzling white speckled with gold flakes, and the mirror above the sink is framed by soft, white spotlights that cast a warm glow. My gaze is drawn to the freestanding shower, boasting a luxurious rainforest shower head that promises a heavenly experience.

“Wow,” I breathe, the word slipping out as I begin to undress, feeling a mix of excitement and nervousness.

“You said the same thing when you walked in last night,” Chase teases, taking a few steps toward the shower. He spins the nozzle, and as the water begins to flow, steam starts to fill the room, wrapping us both in a warm embrace.

We both shower in silence, which I very much appreciate right now.

The hot water and steam cause my headache to fade a little. Chase turns off the shower and steps out first, wrapping a white linen towel around his waist before wrapping one around me.

"Stay, I'll cook us some breakfast".

I nod my head at his suggestion because food sounds fucking good right now. The marble on the kitchen island feels cool as I lean against it, watching Chase open the American style black fridge to grab some breakfast items. I moan as I scoop the scrambled eggs and toast, he makes for us, into my mouth.

"So good. Thank you". He places a small kiss on the side of my face.

"I have a few errands to run today, so please make yourself at home and leave when you're ready" Chase tells me as he walks into the bedroom to get dressed. He pops his head around the door frame for a split second to say, "Or don't. I don't mind".

I roll my eyes as I finish my breakfast and place the dishes into the sink.

"It's okay. I should probably head back to mine." I join Chase and dress myself in last night's clothes. We walk out of his apartment together and part ways as the taxi I booked before we came downstairs pulls up. He nuzzles my nose before pulling open the door and guiding me as I take my seat inside.

My head leans on the leather headrest as I watch people go about their Sunday morning routines. Going to the supermarket, meeting friends at the local cafe, early morning joggers running down the high street.

When I'm with Chase, the world stops. Everything else doesn't seem to matter. Just us. Talking. Laughing. *Fucking.*

I walk up the steps of my apartment and step inside. After brushing my teeth and fresh change of clothes, I water my little plant and face plant my bed. That's where I stay until the next morning when my alarm brings me out of my deep slumber. I begin my weekly work routine of waking up, getting dressed and heading to the office. After starting each day with a morning catch up with the team in the meeting room, I spend most of the week alternating between the café, the gym, and my own office. On Thursday lunchtime, Rain and Skye swing by to join me.

"Hey, girls, won't be a second," I say, glancing up from my laptop to see them waiting at my door. They stroll in, immediately poking around, opening cabinets, flipping through notebooks and files, their curiosity uncontainable. Suddenly, they burst into a fit of giggles, backs turned to me.

"What's so funny?" I ask, shutting my laptop and grabbing my bag from the floor. But I quickly spot the source of their amusement—a stack of sticky notes Chase has left on my desk, each one with some… let's say, very explicit instructions. Blushing, I swipe the notes into a drawer, hoping that's the end of their snooping.

"Come on, let's go get some lunch".

As we step into the café, the enticing aroma of freshly cooked food envelops us. Each table is occupied by small groups of coworkers and friends, taking a break from their day to refuel

We grab plastic trays and load up on salad and meat from the counter. Skye settles into a seat across from Rain and me, her gaze suddenly shifting as she waves at someone walking past our table.

"Afternoon, ladies!" Noah chirps as he strolls by.

"Skye, are you blushing?" I tease, taking a forkful of my salad, which tastes dreadful. Seriously, why can't I eat pizza every day? *Because you're not fourteen anymore, Monica.*

"No, I'm not," she mumbles, fiddling with her food instead of eating. Rain giggles beside me. "Oh yes, you are."

"Jesus, I feel like I'm back in high school," Skye replies, setting her fork down. "It was nice talking to Noah the other night; he likes all the same things I do. We have a lot in common."

Rain and I exchange glances, and she can't help but ask, "Did you tell him you're married?"

"Didn't come up," Skye shrugs, brushing off the question.

We let it slide and turn our focus back to lunch, swapping office gossip and making plans for the weekend, the playful banter filling the air around us.

The day wraps up and I power down my laptop, glad to have successfully completed another day without giving into the temptation of Chase. Even if the sticky notes he leaves me do wild things to my imagination. Sliding my arms through the sleeves of my jacket, my phone pings in my bag. I reach in and see a text message from him.

Mr Marino:

Dinner, tonight, 7pm, my place.

Me:

Is that an offer or another order?

Mr Marino:

Red or white wine?

Me:

Rosé

Mr Marino:

See you tonight.

I step into my apartment, just enough time to shower and slip into something far from work mode. My black knitted sweater dress hugs every curve as I pull it on, and the cool leather of my knee-high boots gives just the right edge. After locking the door, I head down to my car. The engine purrs to life, filling the night air with its rumble. Traffic is light tonight, and before I know it, I'm pulling up to Chase's. When he opens the door, I take him in a crisp white T-shirt, black jeans that fit a little too perfectly, and clean white trainers. I can't decide if I like him all dressed casually or in his sexy office suits. *Well, if we're talking about preferences, I prefer him wearing nothing at all.* He leads me inside, the mouth-watering aroma of garlic and spices swirling around us.

"Dinner smells amazing," I say as he slips my jacket from my shoulders.

"Won't be long until it's ready," he replies, hooking my jacket onto the metal peg by the door. His eyes flick to it, curiosity lighting up his face.

"Alright, tell me—what's the story behind these matching white leather jackets that you, Rain, and Skye have?" I can't help but laugh, memories bubbling up.

"Well… we were inspired by the Pink Ladies from Grease." I caught his eye, waiting for his reaction. His laugh comes easily, genuine, making his eyes crinkle as he shakes his head.

"That's brilliant," he says, grinning. "So, does that mean Jordan, Noah, and I are the T-Birds?".

A smile spreads across my face, and I raise an eyebrow.

"Yeah, maybe."

Chase pulls out a chair for me at his grand wooden dining table, then heads back to the kitchen to plate up the meal. He places a steaming dish of chicken and pasta in a creamy sauce in front of me, and the rich scent alone makes my mouth water. I take a bite, and my eyes go wide at the taste—silky, savoury, with just the right hint of herbs. My eyes flutter closed.

"Wow, Chase, this is incredible."

He just smiles, reaching to fill our glasses with the Rosé wine I requested.

"It's my Nonna's recipe," he says softly.

"You're the first person, besides me and Jordan, that I've made it for." His quiet confession sends a warmth through my chest, and I can feel my heart picking up speed.

"She passed before I was old enough to make it for her." He looks down at his plate, smiling.

I place my hand on top of his, "I'm sure she would've been very proud of you."

We fall into an easy rhythm of talking, laughing, and teasing each other as we savour every bite. When we finish, he gathers our empty plates and disappears into the kitchen, only to return moments later to guide me to his cosy living room. I settle beside him on the couch, swinging my legs across his lap as he browses the streaming options. He settles on an action comedy, but my attention has drifted—I'm not watching the screen; I'm watching him. I know I'm not the first woman to admire Chase—his looks, his drive, the effortless charm he radiates. But out of everyone, he chose me.

Halfway through the film, I noticed Chase staring at my legs. I unzipped my boots and placed them beside me before laying my legs across him. He strokes my legs softly, causing goosebumps to pebble up and down my skin. As he snakes his hand up my inner thigh, I feel his cock tense and press up beneath me.

His brown eyes go wide as I swing myself around him. Leaning forward I push myself down on him as he begins to pepper kisses across my jaw. It doesn't take long before his length hardens even more and presses beneath me. He moans as I drop to my knees before him. Chase leans back against his leather sofa and swings both arms to rest on the back of his head. I slowly undo his jeans and pull down the zipper. His cock springs free in front of my face. I don't know how that fits inside me let alone how I'm going to fit it in my mouth. But a sense of courage envelopes me as I grab the base of him and lick the tip.

"Fuck. That feels so good Monica".

He lets out a deep moan as I close my lips around him. I continue bobbing my head and stroking him with my hands.

"That's it. You are doing so well", my core pulses at his praise. He grabs the back of my head to bring me closer to him causing my eyes water a little, but I carry on.

I don't usually enjoy giving head to guys, but the sounds that are escaping Chase's lips and his praise for me, makes me revel in the moment.

Chase bucks his hips forward as comes, letting out a deep groan as he does. My throat goes warm, and I swallow his release as he zips his jeans back up.

Chase stands and gently pulls me up beside him. He stays silent and I wonder what his next move is going to be.

He grabs his phone from the coffee table, connecting it to the speakers by the TV. Moments later, a gentle melody of guitars and a soft voice singing in Italian fills the room. I watch as he effortlessly moves the coffee table aside, slipping off his shoes as he clears space for us. My toes sink into the soft, plush rug, grounding me in the moment. Then he turns to me, bowing slightly as he extends his hand, inviting me to dance. I place my hand in his, feeling the warmth of his grip as I step closer, pressing gently against him. We sway together, bodies moving to the rhythm, our eyes locked as the world fades away. In this perfect, quiet moment, I can't imagine ever wanting it to end.

•••••••••••••••••••••••••••••••••••

A burst of steam hits my face as I smooth out the last wrinkle in my blush-pink shirt the next morning. My fingers press against the cool metal as I zip up my black pencil skirt and slide on a pair of comfortable, matching pink ballet flats. With a quick coffee in hand, I head down to the car park, where my cherry-red Porsche gleams in the morning light. Sliding into the driver's seat, I place my travel cup snugly in the cupholder, then search the console for my signature red lipstick.

Seriously, I lost another one? I rifle through every nook and cranny until, finally, the glovebox yields my missing lipstick.

As I reach to close it, I notice the folded stack of paperwork Rain held in her hands a few weeks ago. I didn't bother reading it at the time, but curiosity tugs at me now. Leaning back, I unfold it and freeze as I read the words: *Full ownership to Monica Martinez*. My jaw drops. This isn't a company car? It's *mine*? Chase bought this...for *me*?

My foot slams down on the accelerator as I rocket out of the car park, the world outside blurring as I weave through traffic. Tires screech as I skid into a parking spot outside the office building, throwing the door shut behind me with a hard slam.

Without missing a beat, I march inside, make a beeline for the lift, and hit the button for the floor with the meeting room. As the doors open, I spot Chase, and the team already gathered around the table through the glass wall.

I stride down the corridor, pulse racing, and push the door open with a force that catches everyone's attention. Chase's head turns, his expression unreadable as he meets my gaze. I want to storm over to him, grab his face, and press my lips to his. Listen as cheers and whoops erupt around us as I boldly kiss our boss, not caring who knows anymore.

But my legs freeze. I can't move. If everyone found out about us, what would they say? That I'm trying to work my way up in the world by sleeping with the boss? *That I'm desperate?*

Chase's gaze locks on mine for a moment, then he clears his throat. "Well, good morning, Monica." Warmth creeps up my cheeks, and I look down as he shifts his attention back to the team as I awkwardly take a seat at the table.

"As I was saying," he continues smoothly, "we've got an award show coming up in Paris. Just under three months to boost those numbers." I nod along with the team, trying to stay focused, though his deep caramel eyes keep pulling at my attention.

As the meeting wraps up, the team files out, but not before Chase asks me to stay behind. Their voices drop to whispers as the door clicks shut behind them. Chase and I rise from our seats, slowly stepping toward each other. "Hi," he murmurs, reaching to tuck a strand of hair behind my ear.

"Hi," I reply softly, a warmth spreading through me.

"What was the big dramatic entrance about?" He chuckles lightly.

I reach into my leather handbag and dangle the cars in front of us. "I can't believe you bought me a Porsche. Thank you."

His hands glide gently up and down my arms, sending a thrill across my skin.

"The pleasure will be all mine," he says, his voice low and teasing. I smile, rising onto my tiptoes to press a soft kiss to his cheek.

22 CHASE

The way Monica burst into the room, you would have thought the building was on fire, *or that she lost another lipstick*. I was wondering how long it would take her to find out about the car. Once the meeting wraps up and the team filters out, she strides over to me, her eyes sparkling. Standing on her toes, she kisses me, and I can feel the warmth of pride swelling in my chest. She tells me how grateful she is for the car.

This girl deserves the entire world. The perfect husband, with the perfect house, living a perfect life. I shake those soft thoughts from my head.

Monica isn't ready for all that. I'm not ready.

Am I?

After we part, we both head to our respective offices. I push open the door to mine, expecting the usual quiet of the morning, but instead, I find my PR manager Tom already settled into my leather chair, looking far too comfortable. "Good morning, Chase," he says, standing to shake my hand with an easy grin.

"Morning, Tom. To what do I owe the pleasure?" I ask, taking my seat. He reaches into his briefcase and produces a thick white file, a tangible reminder of the work that awaits.

"I'm here to pass along some ideas for Jordan's opening of his new dealership," Tom continues, sliding the file across the table. I can't help but feel a swell of pride knowing I nudged Jordan to work with the same PR firm that's been instrumental in my success.

"No problem, I can get that to him tonight," I assure him, standing to shake his hand before walking him down the noisy corridor towards the lift.

As I stand with my hands tucked into my pockets, I take a moment to survey my team, engrossed in their work, the hum of productivity creating a comforting background. I make a mental note to add a little extra to their Christmas bonuses this year; they've truly earned it.

The day unfolds in a blur of meetings and tasks, but a hint of sadness washes over me when Monica tells me she has plans with Carlos tonight. With a sigh, I pull out my phone and call Jordan, asking him to meet me at the office. An hour later, just as I'm getting lost in thought, there's a knock at my door.

"Hello, brother." Jordan glides in, a casual grin on his face as he takes a seat opposite me.

"Fancy a drink?" He waves a bottle enticingly, and I give him a slow nod, a smile creeping onto my face. Jordan knows me better than anyone.

I walk over to the water machine in the corner of the room, grabbing two plastic cups. As my computer powers down, Jordan begins pouring into the cups, the sound of liquid filling the silence between us. "Saluti," we say in unison, the ritual grounding us in the moment.

"Monica knows about the car". I confess, a hint of mischief slipping into my tone. "I'm in so deep with this girl."

"Well, congratulations," he replies, raising his cup in a toast. His genuine smile and the warmth in his eyes.

"Just don't fuck it up now". I drain the last of my drink and, in a playful jab, toss my cup at Jordan for his snarky comment.

"I won't," I say, the words coming out firmer than I intended. "I care about her. I think she's what I've been looking for. She makes me a better person." God, I feel like a lovestruck teenager, caught off guard by the intensity of it all. Maybe I am ready to settle down?

An ache appears in my chest, but I ignore it as I hand Jordan the file from Tom, watching as he flips through the pages, his expression serious. His eyes flick up and down the pages.

For a moment, I just take it all in. Jordan and I have come so far, each step forward a nod to our parents' dreams.

They left Verona over thirty years ago, hoping for a better life here in the UK—not just for themselves but for us, their sons.

My father poured everything he had into his own business, with my mother by his side, determined to build something from the ground up. When we were finally old enough to stand on our own two feet, they retired and returned to Verona, the place they always called home.

Jordan pauses from reading the files and looks up at me.

"Just remember the terms of our deal, Chase: I only settle down when you do. And trust me, I've still got a few good years of parties, and one-night stands left in me."

I wave a hand dismissively. "Yes, yes, I know. Aren't you getting sick of it by now?"

Jordan shakes his head with a grin.

He's holding on to his playboy lifestyle for as long as he can, and years ago, he roped me into this ridiculous pact: he'd only settle down if I did first. At the time, I didn't think much of it—neither of us were even considering slowing down.

A year ago, I'd have said my priorities were good times and building my businesses. But lately, that life doesn't feel as important to me anymore.

It's frustrating, this sense of being held back by my own promise. The irony isn't lost on me—I'm ready to leave the playboy life behind, but my own words are stopping me.

Still, after a heavy night of drinking a few years ago, we made a pact: he wouldn't settle until I did. And since the Marino brothers don't break promises to each other, we took each other's word as gospel. Loyalty is what's keeping me here, even if my heart's no longer in it.

The bottle slowly empties as the hours slip by. We barely notice how late it's gotten until Jordan orders a taxi, requesting a stop at my place along the way.

I give him a quick hug, bidding him goodnight before heading inside, feeling the quiet of the house wrap around me. My bed is calling, but tonight, the thought of it without Monica feels colder somehow. I decided to sleep on the sofa instead.

•················•················•

The next morning, I meet Monica at the local park for a picnic. Autumn has just settled in, and I take a seat at one of the wooden benches near a semi-circle of blooming flowers, waiting for her. Soon, I spot her on the busy path, weaving through families and couples walking their dogs. My heart races as she approaches, looking radiant in a cream knitted sweater dress and matching boots. She's like an angel, and as she sits across from me, she begins to unpack her tote bag filled with sandwiches, cakes, and sweets.

"What?" she asks, her tone shy, noticing my gaze.

"You look beautiful," I say simply, watching her cheeks flush pink as I lean in to kiss her ruby-red lips.

"I'd like you to come with me to Jordan's dealership opening next week," I tell her as she unwraps some food.

She pauses, her eyes lighting up. "That would be nice; I'd be happy to go with you."

I smile, keeping to myself the fact that my parents will be flying in for the event. I don't want her to feel pressured, but I do want them to meet her.

We relax into conversation, enjoying the spread Monica has prepared. She tells me about Carlos's new girlfriend, Cathay.

"I think he's really happy, which makes me happy," she says, bobbing her head. "I've met her a few times now."

"Do you think it's serious?" I ask, taking a bite of the cream and strawberry cake she brought.

"I don't know. Maybe." She glances around before lowering her voice.

"I saw something weird the other night—" Before she can continue, a man appears at the edge of our table, breathing heavily.

"Hey, guys, how's it going?" It's Noah, hands on his hips and dripping in sweat.

"Oh, hey Noah. Good, thanks," Monica replies politely, clearly surprised.

He grins, ignoring her tone.

"How's Skye?" he asks, clearly fishing for something. He's asked about her sister before, and every time, I tell him to fuck off.

"Erm… she's fine. Busy with work." Monica's voice is tinged with discomfort, and Noah seems to sense it. He gives a quick wave before jogging back down the path.

"That was so weird," Monica giggles, returning to her lunch.

"Yeah, it was" I reply, watching as Noah disappears into the crowd.

"No, it's weird because Skye also goes jogging in this park", her eyebrows rise as she continues chewing her food.

"I think he likes her," I tease.

"She's married… for now." She raises an eyebrow, mischief in her eyes. She tells me about how Skye and her husband met, started a business together, and eventually got married. But from what she shares, Steve never treated Skye as an equal—neither in their work nor in their private life. The idea of Monica and me going from loving working together to not being able to stand each other seems unthinkable. I've seen it work before, though, with my own parents. I know it can work.

We finish up our lunch date and head to The Dog and Gun for a quiet evening drink. The park is conveniently located between our apartments and the pub, but we enjoy the brisk walk together. Monica places her small hand in mine, and we stroll towards her father's pub as a couple. I expect her to let go of my hand as we reach the pub, but she doesn't. Carlos's eyes go wide as we walk in, but his expression forms a grin. My heart beats slow a little. I don't want to piss him off but equally, Monica is a grown woman and can make her own choices. I extend my hand over the bar to greet him, and he does the same. Monica reaches on her tiptoes and places a kiss on his cheek. My heart flutters at how much she adores her father, just how I adore mine.

"Take a seat. I'll bring some drinks over".

We both nod and find a free table towards a quiet corner of the pub. Within a few minutes Carlos brings over two full glasses of red wine. He takes a seat next to his daughter, kisses the side of her head and throws his muscled arm around her. His lips form a flat smile, but he squints his dark brown eyes at me.

Carlos gives me the impression that he's happy to see us together, but I can't help but feel a little intimidated right now.

23 MONICA

It had been over a week since Chase, my dad, and I had sat together for drinks, a moment that had brought me reassurance. The atmosphere was tense at first, but I quickly broke the ice with a light-hearted lie about losing yet another lipstick. It was just the distraction I needed to get the two cavemen before me to stop squinting at each other. I let out a deep sigh when they both burst into laughter, and the mood began to lift.

Chase filled my dad in on Jordan's new dealership celebration party happening this weekend and our upcoming trip to Paris. After detailing his current office locations and ambitious expansion plans, my dad decided to chime in with a playful jab. "Seems you've done a lot of travelling, Chase. Any hidden families tucked away anywhere?"

Chase's face flushed bright red, and he chuckled, "No sir."

I couldn't help but elbow my dad in the ribs, amused by his cheeky sense of humour. That evening ended with my dad introducing Cathay to Chase. She spoke about how she started the café to support her three boys when they were young, and she can hardly believe that the Willow Café is about to celebrate its 20th anniversary. Both she and my dad take great pride in their businesses, but I can't help but worry that she might hurt him. We've both endured enough heartbreak caused by women to last a lifetime.

The day of Jordan's launch finally arrives, and I head to Chase's apartment to get ready. After a hot shower, I step out of the bathroom, wrapped in one of his soft cotton towels. He's sprawled across the bed wearing nothing but a pair of black Calvin Klein boxers, watching me intently, his gaze warm and unwavering. Smirking, I pull out my makeup bag from my overnight bag.

"What are you staring at?" I tease, a playful glint in my eye.

He doesn't respond, just shifts closer, moving to the edge of the bed where I'm standing, trying to get dressed for the evening. Even as I'm standing there and him seated, his frame towers over me, casting a shadow that makes me feel like a small flower beneath the shelter of a tall, steady tree. Chase grabs the sides of the towel and drops it, exposing my tits. He wets his bottom lip with his tongue, causing my core to pulse. My nipples pucker as Chase brings them to his mouth, sucking them so hard, goosebumps pebble across my skin.

His hands cup my naked body as I swing my legs around his waist. I kiss his stubbled jaw as he licks at my neck and moans.

"Mr Marino, I think I'm addicted to you". I tell him as I grind against his hard length beneath me. His lips grazed my ear as he began to speak, "Monica,".

I think that's one of the few times he's used my name, and not 'Cherry' whilst we're alone.

"I think I'm falling for you".

The room goes silent and all I hear are our rapid breaths as I stare intensely into his eyes. Hope, heartbreak, home, love, care, passion, obsession, are all the things I see in his eyes when he looks at me.

"I think… I'm falling for you too Chase".

The next few seconds blur as he turns his body with me still wrapped around him, slams me onto his satin red bed sheets. My head hits the pillow, and my black curls spread across my bare shoulders. He slowly spreads my trembling legs, kissing the inside of my thighs as he hooks one leg over his left shoulder, giving him deeper access and bringing him closer to me. His tongue swipes upwards along my clit, causing me to buck my hips towards him. Slowly, he pushes two fingers inside me and begins pumping fast, whilst continuing to swirl his tongue along my throbbing core. A deep moan escapes my mouth.

"Chase…".

My breathing turns into rapid panting.

"That's my girl".

His praise causes me to completely shatter around him.

Chase appears from between my legs to place a kiss on my lips, my chest rising and falling fast as he looms over me, looking deeply into my eyes and a smirk spread across his lips. Chase lifts me from the mattress onto my bare feet. After catching my breath, I take small steps to enter the bathroom to wash and get dressed for Jordan's party. An hour passes by and Chase tells me that our driver is waiting downstairs. The cool evening air slams into the skin on my legs, causing goosebumps to pebble. Chase notices and brings me closer to him as a black limousine pulls up. My eyes go wide.

"You said we were getting a taxi, as in a *car*?" I ask Chase as he grips the door handle, opening the door to guide me inside.

"This is a taxi- it's just *this* taxi has champagne on ice".

I roll my eyes at him as he takes the seat next to me and the vehicle begins to move. Music flows through the back of the limo as Chase pops open the bottle of champagne that's sitting on a bucket of ice. The bubbles fizz up my nose as I take a small sip. It tastes…*expensive.*

The driver raps his knuckles three times on the blacked-out divider causing me to jump a little.

"What does *that* mean?"

"It means we have thirty minutes," Chase whispers as he inches closer to me. He takes the empty flute from my hand and places it next to his on the black tray beside him. For the second time this evening I swing my legs around him and push my signature silver dress above my waist. Except tonight, I'm trying something new.

"Monica, are you trying to kill me?"

I look at him with complete innocence. "What?" I whisper in his ear, as I tug on his ear lobe.

"You're not wearing anything under…".

Chase moves at lightning speed to undo his leather belt. He moves his trousers and boxers down, and his cock springs free. I wet my bottom lip with my tongue as I climb on top of him and relax my weight. The vehicle's tires roll over speed bumps causing me and Chase to move closer each time. My core throbs from the friction and I'm so close to coming again.

Chase knows my body now, better than I do, and notices my breathing getting faster. He flicks his thumb over my clit, driving me over the edge. He bucks his hips faster as he comes. We stay motionless, breathing each other's air as the limp begins to slow down. I climb off him and pull my dress down as he zips up his trousers and buckles his belt. I feel the wetness running down my legs as I shift back into my seat. We both let out a breathy laugh as the driver knocks three times again on the divider, alerting us of our arrival.

As we hop out of the limo, Jordan is there to greet us, guiding us toward the entrance of the grand showroom. The main glass doors are decked out with a cool arch of gold and black balloons, and music blares from huge speakers, setting a lively vibe as we walk in. Every car inside is decked out with stickers, confetti, and banners, making the place feel like a party. I spot Chase smiling proudly at his brother, mingling with the crowd.

I turn and stand on my toes, meeting Chase halfway as he leans down for a kiss. Just then, a cough from behind pulls us out of our moment.

We turn to see a tall man with dark skin, a neatly trimmed beard, and a black tuxedo standing before us. Beside him is a slightly shorter woman with dark, curly hair, bronze skin, piercing brown eyes, and a sleek, dark purple pantsuit. Chase greets the couple warmly, pulling them both into a hug just as Jordan walks over to join us.

Please don't tell me I'm meeting Chase's parents with come dripping down my thighs.

"Monica, this is my mother, Sofia, and my father, Leonardo." My body freezes; suddenly, I can't remember how to speak or move.

"Madre e Padre, this is Monica." He gestures from them to me, and as I extend my hand to greet them, it trembles slightly. His parents exchange a knowing glance before his mother pulls me into a warm embrace, quickly followed by his father.

As I step back to stand next to Chase, his mother chuckles softly.

"Welcome to the family." Her thick accent wraps around her words as she gently strokes the sleeves of her husband's jacket. "It's so lovely to see my boy has settled down."

An awkward laugh escapes me, and I catch Chase rolling his eyes at his mother.

Just then, Jordan saves the moment by suggesting, "Well, shall we get some drinks?"

Their parents follow Jordan as he leads them to a pop-up bar in the corner of the showroom. Chase and I linger behind, our footsteps echoing off the tiled floor, though all I can really hear is the thudding of my own heartbeat.

"Chase, why didn't you tell me your parents were coming?" My voice comes out sharper than I intended, betraying the rising panic in my chest. I wait, bracing myself for his answer.

He stops, turning to look at me, his expression calm.

"Because you were already nervous about tonight. And if I'd told you they were here, you'd have been even more nervous."

I feel a prickling heat rise through me, a mix of anger and anxiety. *How could he just decide that for me?* I realise my hands have clenched into fists, nails pressing into my palms, grounding me against the sudden rush of emotions.

I draw in a slow breath, trying to push down the wave of frustration. Then, forcing a composed smile, I nod.

"Fine." I turn and start towards the bar, ignoring the tightness in my chest and the way my stomach flips with every step.

A few moments later, I hear Chase's footsteps as he finally follows, though I don't dare look back.

Jordan has shots lined up along the bar, and I grab one, feeling the burn of the alcohol as it sears down my throat.

Like my body isn't already on fire. I reach for another, downing it even faster, desperate to drown out the pulsing mix of nerves and frustration.

As my hand reaches for a third, Chase's firm grip catches my elbow. His narrowed eyes meet mine, silently warning me to stop.

I shrug his hand off, keeping it subtle to avoid drawing attention, but inside I'm fuming. He has no right to control me.

Meeting his gaze, I tip back the shot defiantly, even running my tongue along the rim of the glass to catch the last drop. Jordan and a few of his coworker's cheer as I slam the glass down, grinning as the warmth spreads through me.

As the night unfolds, the energy around us grows wild—people are laughing, dancing, champagne spraying through the air in sticky arcs. I watch it all through a blur as I sip on my vodka lemonade, the room tilting just enough to feel detached. Chase stands beside me, talking to Jordan, but we haven't exchanged a word all night. I have no idea what I'd even say.

Then, maybe out of defiance, maybe out of pure recklessness, my favourite song blasts through the speakers. Without thinking, I set down my drink, turn to Jordan, and grab his tie, pulling him into the makeshift dance floor that's formed in the centre of the showroom. I see Chase's gaze boring into me, his jaw likely clenched, nostrils flaring, but I don't care.

Jordan and I sway closer, the beat pulsing through us, and I let myself get lost in the music, in the moment, feeling the weight of Chase's stare but refusing to let it pull me back.

I'm not a petty person but right now the anger and alcohol in my body mix and I can't help but revel in how much this is making Chase jealous.

Jordan slips his hand around my waist and it's the last thing I feel before Chase comes storming over. He pushes us apart slowly, snaring at Jordan and telling him to fuck off. Jordan spins on his heels and moves closer to a blonde dancing at the edge of the dancefloor.

Chase snakes his hands around my ass and whispers into my ear, "You're mine Cherry, not his. I'm the only one who touches you like that".

I take a step back, wobbling a little on the balls of my feet and glare up at the man who has completely flipped my world upside down.

24 CHASE

Fear, anger, love, lust, hate—it's all there, blazing in Monica's eyes as she stands glaring up at me. Everyone around us fades into the background; the music mutes, and every sense sharpens as I tell her she's mine. No one—not even my fucking brother—gets to touch her. It's my come drying between her thighs, my name she screams when I'm inside her, my heart that bears her mark.

She's drunk; I can tell she's swaying, unsteady on her feet.

I pull her into my arms, and she slumps against me, mumbling, "Not cool, Chase. You should have told me your parents would be here tonight." Her eyes are a little glassy as she pulls away from my chest, and my body aches at the loss of her warmth.

"I know. I'm sorry." I wrap my hand around her delicate fingers.

"Especially when I'm not wearing any *fucking* underwear." Her hand flies to her mouth and her face goes bright red as she realises, she's just announced that to the entire dancefloor. She hasn't been this anxious in ages, and it kills me to know I caused it. I gently lower her hand and give her a reassuring smile.

"Come on, let's go home."

She hesitates. "What about your parents?"

"They left an hour ago. They asked if we'd like to meet them for breakfast tomorrow."

She hums thoughtfully, then nods. "Thanks for telling me *this* time."

As she turns to walk ahead, I give her a playful slap on the ass, grinning at her sassy reply.

•·················•·················•

We both wake up early on Sunday. Our legs tangled up in the sheets as the TV played one of her favourite shows. Monica has her head resting on my chest, her black curls are splayed across my tattoo, blending in with the ink. It just shows how well we blend. She sits up to take a sip of water and I run my fingers down her bare back causing goosebumps to appear. She twists slightly to throw a smirk over her shoulder.

"Good morning, Mr Marino" she teases. Continuing to stroke her back with one hand, I use the other to check my phone and realise that we're going to be late meeting my parents for breakfast.

I make my way to the bathroom and turn on the shower. I return to the bed and scoop Monica up in my arms, she squeals like a child until I set her down on her feet.

She stands in front of me, steam filling the room from the overhead shower.

"Turn and place your palms flat on the wall".

Her thighs clench together but she obeys and turns. I slide my middle finger down her ass and into her pussy. She's soaking wet when I pull my fingers out. I grip my throbbing cock with my right hand and pump a few times before slamming myself into her. She lets out a deep moan that echoes around the room. My fingers grip her hips hard as I slide in and out of her.

"Chase, I'm so close".

"Beg for it" I tease her by stopping for a split second.

Monica's legs tremble as she turns her head to tell me, "Please". Her begging drives me crazy.

I stop again and feel a smirk spread across my lips. Monica's breaths leave her mouth rapidly.

"Please, don't stop".

I twist my arm under her and flick her clit a few times, driving her over the edge and she screams my name.

"Be as loud as you can Cherry".

She screams my name again as her legs struggle to hold the weight of her body. The sight and the sounds drive my release to the surface, and I see my fingernails mark her ass as I pull out and shoot my come all over bare soaking wet back.

I guide her to straighten, gently tipping her chin so her gaze meets mine. I run my hands along her body, lathering every inch with soap, feeling her soft skin warm under my touch as she mirrors my movements, her fingers tracing slow, tender circles across my chest. The air between us thickens with the scent of her, mingling with the steam.

As much as I enjoy having sex with Monica, bending and breaking her to my will, I love how intimate it feels to wash her body.

I turn off the shower, reluctant to break this moment but knowing we should. We step out, the cool air a stark contrast, and I wrap her in a towel, taking a moment to soak in the sight of her. We get dressed in comfortable silence, a lingering sense of intimacy still hanging between us as we head downstairs. I grab the keys, and we slip into my BMW.

As we step into the restaurant, I spot my parents and Jordan seated at a table in the centre of the room. Glasses of fresh fruit juice, plates of sweet pastries, and baskets of warm bread await us as we make our way over. The sight of Monica hugging my mother tugs at something deep in my chest. My mum's exactly the kind of Mother Monica deserves—warm, always present, a steady light for my dad, Jordan, and me.

I kiss my mum's soft hand, then shake my dad's, feeling his familiar firm grip. Jordan greets me with a punch to the shoulder, which I'm quick to return.

"Don't you two ever behave?" my mum and Monica say at the same time, sharing a look before bursting into laughter.

I can't help but smile; this moment feels perfect. I've never brought anyone home to meet my parents before, and now I'm glad I waited—nothing could ever compare to this. My dad just smirks, settling into his chair, and we all follow suit as the waiter arrives to take our breakfast orders.

My parents chose this spot because it reminds them of home. Shelves filled with Italian wine line the walls, paintings of Italian landmarks add a warm touch, and the tables are dressed in classic red-and-white chequered cloths. It's cosy and familiar, and for once, I feel like everything's exactly as it should be.

Food and conversation flow easily through the afternoon, and after a round of hugs, I watch my parents head off with Jordan, who's taking them to the airport for their flight back to Verona. Slipping my hand into Monica's, I feel her fingers lace through mine as we walk back to my car. She glances up, her red lips curling into a playful smile as she swings our hands together.

"Your parents are nice Chase. You're so lucky to have such a loving and caring mum too".

"My mums great, she can be interfering when she wants to be. My dad can be a little tough at times too, but they've always been there for me and Jordan".

"They're lucky to have you both".

My feet freeze in place as I stop Monica for a moment and crash my lips onto hers.

"I'm lucky to have you". I confess to her.

It hits me then—I haven't just fallen for her. I'm in *love* with her.

25 CHASE

I start the week by firing off a thank-you email to Tom's office for their help with Jordan's showroom launch. I've been spending nearly every evening with Monica lately, and my work has piled up as a result. My head throbs, my shoulders are tight, but I manage to grind through meetings, client calls, and a mountain of contracts that need reviewing and signing.

Jane stops by, setting a fresh coffee on my desk. "Anything else, Chase?" she asks before turning to leave.

Without glancing up from my laptop, I reply, "That's Mr. Marino to you, Jane."

She pauses, an amused look flickering in her eyes. "Oh, well, I just thought… since Monica—"

My jaw tightens. "You thought wrong. Leave her out of this."

Her mouth drops open slightly.

"You can't talk to me like that!" Her voice rises, clearly trying to make a point. Fine—if she wants a scene, she'll get one.

I raise my voice just enough. "I can talk to you however I damn well please. I'm your boss."

"You wouldn't talk to Monica like that," she retorts, arms crossed, and eyebrows raised.

I've had enough. I'm done with her attitude, her lingering glances.

"Get out, Jane," I snap, my patience threadbare.

"I haven't even set foot in your office."

I stand, meeting her gaze from across the room, every word clear.

"No, Jane—get out of my building. You're fired."

I walk over and open my office door, finding my team hovering in their doorways, glancing from Jane to me with expressions of shock and confusion. I've never fired anyone so openly before—it's always been behind closed doors. But today, I'd reached my breaking point.

Monica is the last to emerge, watching me from down the hall. Her expression isn't shocked or confused like the others. It's disappointing. And somehow, that stings more than anger ever could. My chest tightens as I close the door, retreating into my office. I pace to the window, fists clenched, glaring out over the city skyline, my mind still simmering. The anger I'd managed to bury months ago rises again, relentless. *I need to cool down.*

A soft knock pulls me back. The door cracks open, and Monica peers in.

"Hey... everything okay?" Her voice is careful, gentle.

"Fine. I just need a second." I don't turn to face her; I know I can't handle the look on her face.

"Oh… okay. I just thought—"

"What is it with everyone 'thinking' today?" The words shoot out before I can catch them. "I don't pay you to sit around thinking all day—I pay you to do your *fucking* job!"

The silence that follows is sharp, and regret begins to creep in almost instantly. *Well done Chase.*

Monica closes the door without saying a word.

It's late by the time I finish up for the day, locking my office door behind me. The building is quiet—everyone's gone home—except for one soft light still glowing down the hallway. Monica's office.

I make my way down the corridor, moving quietly, and pause outside her window. I can hear her on the phone, she's whispering, but it's Rain's voice coming through the speaker that grabs my attention.

"He fired her?".

"Woah, what a dick."

"He said *what* to you?".

"What an arsehole".

My stomach twists at hearing her friend's blunt assessment of me, but I can't seem to pull myself away. I listen as Monica sighs.

"I think he's just stressed out, I don't know what's gotten into him today, but I'm going home tonight."

A dull ache settles in my chest at the thought of sleeping alone, but if that's what she needs, I won't stop her.

I start heading toward the lift when I hear her office light click off and the door open. She steps out, hand on her chest, startled.

"Oh my god, Chase—you scared me! I thought you'd gone home."

I give her a small, apologetic smile.

"Sorry, I was just finishing up some contracts." The lie slips out easily, though in truth, I've spent the night sitting in my office, feeling sorry for myself. Stubbornly refusing to leave, like a teenager sulking after being told off.

"Oh. I'm going home." she admits.

"Okay, I'll see you tomorrow." I have no idea what I'm supposed to say to her. She looks at me like I've done something wrong—*again.*

The lift ride down to the car park is thick with silence, every second dragging. She disappears into the shadows, heading toward her car without a backward glance. The car park is deserted, just like I feel. Hollow.

The next morning, I'm up early, determined to keep yesterday where it belongs. I kick off my day with a boxing session with Noah at the gym.

"Hold the bag, Noah," I say, throwing a quick one-two jab.

He scoffs, "Mate, I'm trying here."

I slow my breathing, standing up straighter as Noah locks eyes with me.

"What happened yesterday, Chase?"

A long sigh escapes me. "Something I should've done a long time ago." I bite down on my gloves, tugging them off.

"I'm trying to get my head around everything—working with Monica, keeping my workload in check, keeping the clients and you a lot happy. But I'm dealing with it."

Noah's gaze narrows, sceptical.

"If you're dealing with it, then yesterday can't happen again," he says, raising his hands defensively. "Just friendly advice."

My teeth ache from clenching my jaw. I relax my shoulders and bring him in for a hug.

"Thanks bro".

Noah claps me on the shoulders—hard enough to remind me they're sore—but he's grinning, as usual. Over the past few years, he's become a solid mate to me and Jordan. He's like a brother, maybe a bit too intense sometimes, but loyal and hardworking.

We head to the locker room, grab a quick shower, suit up, and head to the office.

As I walk in, I spot Jane packing up her desk. I don't even bother saying anything; I don't feel a shred of guilt for what I did yesterday. Instead, my gaze drifts to Monica's office. She's sitting there, blowing on her travel mug, hands wrapped around it. Thank god she didn't quit. I rap lightly on her door, and when she calls me in, I close the door behind me, leaning against the glass. Monica leaves her chair to stand opposite me, leaning against her desk. She looks tired, a bit sad, like she's about to say something, but I jump in first.

"Hang on—I need to apologise for yesterday."

"Alright," she says, crossing her arms with an edge to her expression.

"I'm sorry if what I did and said upset you," I tell her, standing my ground. "But Jane had it coming."

Monica's eyes narrow.

"Chase, you humiliated her in front of everyone. You owe *her* the apology, not me."

"I'm not apologising to her," I reply, voice steady. "But I will handle situations like that better in the future, and I won't ever speak to you like that again. I promise." And I mean it—I don't make promises I don't plan to keep.

She sighs, clearly still annoyed, but then steps closer, her fingers brushing my arm. "Why did you fire her?"

"She was slacking, and I was fed up with the attitude," I say, pulling her closer. At first, Monica is a bit tense, but then she relaxes into me.

"I missed you," I murmur as I nuzzle my nose against hers.

Her expression softens. "I missed you too."

As Monica leans into me, her perfume drifts up—soft and floral, like spring itself. Her warmth presses against my chest, grounding me. I tilt her chin up gently and graze her lower lip with mine, feeling her shiver slightly. Her cheeks flush, and I can tell she's wary of anyone catching us. But me? I don't give a fuck.

I pull back, giving her a grin, then turn to lower the blinds on her door. She watches, eyes widening slightly as she realises what I'm doing.

"Chase…" she murmurs, but I press a finger to her lips, cutting off any protest. Words aren't what she needs right now; actions speak louder.

I scoop her up and gently settle her on her desk, nudging her files and laptop aside to make space. She leans back, resting on her palms, her gaze dark with anticipation.

Her thighs press together nervously, but I gently part them, my fingers tracing the fabric of her sleek black trousers as I undo the button and slide down the zip. Slowly, I work the trousers down her legs, taking in every inch of her skin as I go.

When I slip her lace underwear down, her body reacts to my touch, and a flicker of a smile crosses her face as I drop to my knees before her. Her wetness glistens in the light.

"Let me show you just how sorry I am," I murmur, voice low. Her hands slip into my hair as I lean in, my lips and tongue trace her pussy, causing her breath to hitch. The world outside fades away, and all that matters now is showing her exactly how much she means to me, no words necessary.

26 MONICA

Chase leaves my office, smirking like the damn Cheshire cat, leaving a trail of trouble in his wake. In just a few short weeks, I've shattered every rule I've ever set for myself—and it's all because of him. I say *I* because, let's be honest, I have absolutely no control when it comes to Chase.

What he did yesterday hurt, not only because of what he put Jane through, but because of the raw, feral look in his eyes as he did it. I feel like Chase is hiding the real reason he fired Jane, but after yesterday's events, I've learnt better than to press him when he's not ready to talk. I've forgiven him for the way he spoke to me. After all, he did apologise in more ways than one.

I blame that damn accent of his. Drawing me in, in more ways than one.

The day wraps up quickly and I whip my phone from my pocket and message the group chat with Rain and Skye. I'm in desperate need of a wine and pamper night.

Me:

Wine, facemasks, pizza, cheesy romance movies tonight at mine?

Rain (Bestie):

I'm down! See you tonight

Skye:

As long as we have wine, I'll be there

I let out a deep breath as the lift descended, carrying me down to my Porsche parked below. After a quick stop at the supermarket to grab dinner for me and the girls, I swung by my dad's place to snag a couple of bottles of his finest red wine.

"Hey, Papi," I greeted, spotting him behind the bar, slicing open cardboard boxes with Cathay by his side. She's been lending him a hand during the busier evening shifts.

"Hello, muñeca," he grinned, rolling his eyes playfully toward his new girlfriend.

Cathay turned from her perch on the ladder, her curly blonde hair swishing as she arranged bottles on the top shelf. "Hi, sweetheart! How are you? Your dad mentioned you'd be stopping by, so I tucked a couple of bottles of the good stuff behind the bar." She winked, handing me the wine.

"Thanks, Cathay! See you!"

A chill creeps over me as I slip back into my car, so I turned on the heated seats and smiled to myself, reflecting on how much my life had changed in the last few weeks—and how, for once, I wouldn't change a thing.

•.................•.................•

A few hours later, I'm showered, wrapped up in comfy clothes, and surrounded by my best friends in front of the TV. A cheesy romance flick plays, though none of us are really watching. We're camped out around the coffee table, sharing pizza slices and sipping wine, laughing over anything and everything. Rain giggles as she shows Skye and me the ridiculous memes Jordan sends her, and I can't help but root for something to spark between them.

"So, you two are just friends? Nothing else?" I tease, waggling my eyebrows.

She smirks and shakes her head.

"We just get on well. Same humour and all. But I'm not interested like that." She flips her phone face-down on the table. "Besides, I could never compete with his lineup of drop dead gorgeous one-night stands."

Skye and I exchange a glance. "And how would you know what they look like?" I ask.

"Come on, Rain, it's not like he's sending you pictures," Skye teases with a smirk.

"Well… actually, he kind of is," Rain admits with a shrug, a slight smile tugging at her lips.

"He keeps sending me screenshots from the dating app and asks if I can, you know, 'read their auras.'" She raises her fingers in air quotes, rolling her eyes.

Skye laughs. "And what do you tell him?"

"I keep saying, 'It doesn't work like that!' I'm just a really good judge of character," Rain replies, a hint of exasperation in her voice.

Skye and I share another look. Maybe they really are just friends. We all prop our elbows on the sofa cushions we've tossed onto the floor, getting cosy for a long night of gossip and drinks. Skye's jaw drops as I spill every detail of what went down yesterday with Chase and Jane.

"If he ever hurts you, I'll kill him," she says, stabbing fiercely at the slice of pizza on her plate.

I burst out laughing. "Okay… but who hurt *you*?"

Rain, sitting next to her, gently removes the fork from Skye's clenched fist, her expression half-amused, half-worried.

"No one. I'm just stating a fact." Skye exhales, her breath escaping like it had been bottled up for ages. She takes a sip of wine, then refills my glass and Rain's before cradling her own. After a pause, she finally lowers her gaze and murmurs, "I think Steve is cheating on me."

The words hang in the air, and I feel my chest tighten as a tear slips down her flushed cheek. Rain rests her head on Skye's shoulder, while I take Skye's hand in mine, giving it a reassuring squeeze.

She shares how Steve has been working away more, coming home with shirts she doesn't recognise in his weekend bag, and even locking his phone in a drawer at night. My heart clenches for Skye.

"Is this why you've been talking to my dad so much?" I ask softly.

She nods, a small smile tugging at her lips.

"Carlos has been amazing, Mon." She wipes her nose on the sleeve of her grey sweater. "He says I'm probably overthinking things and that I should talk to Steve about it. But, between us… maybe this is the perfect reason to leave him."

Rain and I exchange wide-eyed glances, jaws dropping.

"What do you mean, leave him?" Rain asks.

Skye waves her hand dismissively.

"That's a story for another night. I don't want to ruin the vibe. Now, who's ready for another bottle of wine?"

A few rounds of board games follow, and laughter fills the room every time Rain sends the dice flying off the board. I scoop up the dice for my turn, but the intercom buzzer interrupts us. I shrug, standing to answer.

"Hello," I sing, voice tinged with the pleasant fog of wine.

"It's Chase."

I press the button to unlock the door, and soon hear his heavy footsteps on the stairs. As he approaches, I spot a bouquet of red roses in his hands. I reach out, but he pulls them back, his eyes glinting with mischief.

"Not so fast," he says. "Kiss first, flowers second."

I lean in, savouring the floral scent before wrapping my arms around him, breathing in his aftershave.

"I was sitting in my car, thinking about all the things I want to do to—"

I cut him off quickly, gesturing towards Rain and Skye who are barely containing their laughter.

"Erm… at work next week," he amends, his face flushing red for a change.

I smirk. "Sure, send me an email, yeah? See you on Monday, boss." I throw him a wink as he heads back down the stairs, my hand still tingling from his touch.

I squeal, practically skipping to the kitchen to replace the sad, wilted roses that Chase gave me a few weeks ago with my new, fresh bouquet. I tip out the old water, refill the vase, and arrange the fresh roses, grinning so hard my cheeks start to ache. Back at the table, I catch Rain giving me a dreamy, love-struck look, while Skye watches me with a mix of happiness and sadness. When was the last time Steve had bought flowers for her?

Frowning, I head back to the kitchen, carefully removing two roses from the bunch. One of the thorns pricks my finger, but I ignore it and return to the table, taking a small bow before presenting each rose to Rain and Skye. Rain pulls hers close, practically burying her face in the petals as if she might just take a bite. Skye, on the other hand, softens, her expression melting into a genuine, full-blown smile.

27 CHASE

Preparation for the awards show is in full swing; the only thing left on my checklist is writing my speech. Tom insisted I prepare two versions—one for if I win and one for if I don't. But I knew there was no need for the latter. I was confident that Be Creative would walk away with another trophy to add to my wall.

It was late one night, and I was still working in my office when Monica surprised me with dinner. The aroma of herbs and spices drifted down the corridor, making my stomach growl before I even saw the pizza box. I smiled as she walked in, and I quickly moved my laptop aside to make room for the paper plates and napkins she'd brought too.

"How's the speech coming along?" she asked, licking a spot of sauce from her finger after taking a slice of pizza from the box. I get lost in the memory of when Monica dropped to her knees in front of me. Taking my cock like the good girl she is. Sucking back and forth. My cock strains against my trousers. She stares at me and I realise I hadn't answered her question.

"Oh, fine. Nearly done," I lie. If I tell her I haven't even started, she'll just push me to get it finished. But, right now I want to enjoy having dinner with my girl. Monica nods, still chewing her food, seemingly satisfied. I grab a slice straight from the box and take a huge bite, not bothering with a plate. She huffs a laugh and rolls her eyes.

The week before last Tom reached out to me to let me know that he had organised the travel to France and booked the most ridiculously priced hotel he could find. The whole team would be heading to the award show including Jane's replacement. Jake joined a few weeks ago—fresh out of university, brimming with energy, and definitely not interested in me. The slight sass in his stride during his interview was a dead giveaway that I'm absolutely *not* his type. Despite his tendency to call me "babe" (a habit I've had to correct more than once), his work ethic and attitude are exactly what I need on this team. We both sink back into our chairs, and Monica starts filling me in on her week. These quiet, everyday moments make me wonder if I could do this every night—sharing dinner, swapping stories, working side by side. What if I asked her to be my business partner? Would she say yes?

As we wrap up the night going over her notes for the award show, I notice Monica stifling a yawn, her eyes drooping with exhaustion. She needs sleep, but selfishly, I'm not ready for this evening to end. Reaching across the desk, I gently take the thick notebook from her hands and slip it into the drawer beside my stack of sticky notes. She gives me a puzzled look, and I can't help but smile.

"Let's go for a drive. I want to show you something," I say, leaning over so she can hear the quiet excitement in my voice.

"Okay," she whispers, her lips curving into a soft grin.

I flick off the lights and close the office door with a gentle click. As we step out, I drape my arm around her shoulders, drawing her in close enough to catch the sweet, familiar scent of her berry shampoo. She always smells and looks like a goddamn dessert, like the cherry on top of a cake. Monica glances up at me, her eyes sparkling in the low light.

Outside, the night wraps around us, thick and dark, with only the distant glow of street lamps breaking through. We slide into my car, and she settles into the seat next to me, her hand resting on the console, just inches from mine. The engine roars softly as I turn the key, and with a swift glance to make sure she's ready, I press down on the accelerator. The tires screech as we pull out of the car park, the headlights carving a path through the inky darkness.

"So, where are we going?" She turns towards me, her knees brushing against each other. I let one hand leave the steering wheel to slip between her warm thighs.

"If I told you, it wouldn't be a surprise now, would it?"

She pouts, her bottom lip jutting out, and I can't help but reach over, gently tugging it. She lets out a playful squeal, retreating just a little.

The drive is short, and I pull my BMW to a stop at the top of a secluded hill, hidden by trees. We're perched right where the city blurs into the countryside, and the view is… breathtaking. Jordan and I used to ride our bikes up here every summer as kids. We'd pedal for hours, pushing our bikes to the limit until they finally gave out. When they did, we left them here, rusting under the sun, and never bothered to replace them. Deep down, we both knew it just wouldn't feel the same. I didn't have a reason to come back here, until now.

As I turn off the engine, I glance at Monica. Her eyes go wide, captivated by the sight. The city lights, softened by the evening mist, look as if they're smouldering, like the whole skyline's aflame. It's how I feel whenever Monica touches me—like my entire body is on fire. And in this moment, I know I'd set the world on fire if anyone tried to hurt her.

"Chase…this is…" She unbuckles her seatbelt, leaning forward to take in the view in front of us, her breath catching.

"I know," I say, unbuckling my own seatbelt to lean closer. "It's one of my favourite places in the city".

She leans back in her seat, turning her attention to me.

"When did you move to Manchester?"

I glanced out at the skyline, the city lights stretching far into the distance. It always looked peaceful from up here, like the chaos didn't exist.

"Jordan and I were born in Verona,"
I said, my voice low, almost drowned out by the hum of cars driving by behind us.

"I was five when our parents decided to pack up everything and move us here. Jordan was seven, old enough to complain about leaving his friends behind, but we didn't have a choice."
I ran a hand through my hair, a half-smile tugging at my lips.

"They wanted to start a business together, something they could build from scratch. And they did. They worked themselves to the bone for years, made sure we had everything we needed. Then, once Jordan and I were sorted, they retired and moved back to Verona."

I shrugged, the smile lingering. "But the accent? That's not going anywhere."

She glances back at me, a soft smile lighting up her face.

"Tell me about your childhood my love".
She takes a deep breath in.

"So my mum and dad met when my mother went on holiday with her sister to Spain. She met my dad on the beach one day when he accidently threw a beach ball at her. They spent the rest of the week together. He promised to come back the year after and he did. Then it went from there. He left everything behind and moved to Manchester to be with my mum. But my mum hid her drinking problem from him."
I reach over to take her small hand in mine.

"She stopped drinking when she fell pregnant with me. But as soon as I was born, she went back to drinking all day and all night.

One day she packed her bag and left. I haven't heard from her since. Nor do I want to. Me and dad are happy as we are".

I watch her shoulders drop down and I feel like she needed to get last part off her chest. Her admitting it out loud releases that heaviness that she's been carrying.

We're lost in each other's gaze, the world fading away until her eyelids start to droop, and she finally closes them. I reach behind me to grab my jacket that's sitting on the back seat and cover her body with it. Gently, I brush a finger along her cheek and whisper, "I love you."

She drifts off to sleep, and I sit there, watching her peaceful face until sleep claims me too.

•·················•·················•

The sun rises early, casting warm rays through the windscreen. I blink awake to find Monica's eyes already on me, her smile soft and sleepy.

"We accidentally fell asleep," she murmurs, a little laugh in her voice.

"Looks like we did. Fancy grabbing some breakfast?"

She nods, fastening her seatbelt. I clip mine in as well, start the car, and we head down the hill, ready to start our Saturday morning together.

I park up round the corner from a bakery and step out of the car, quickly making my way to Monica's side to open the door for her, wondering when I suddenly became so chivalrous.

The streets are busy, people shopping and meeting friends for breakfast, but I keep her close as she places her cold hand into mine. I instantly feel her skin warm from my touch. There's a fresh chill in the air which makes us pick up our speed to head inside to the bakery.

The bell above the door rings as I hold open the glass door for Monica to walk through, but she freezes.

"Chase," She glares up at me, with a twinkle in her eye.

"Yes, amore mio?"

A few seconds of silence by pass.

"I love you too".

28 MONICA

I pull the phone away from my ear as Rain squeals down the phone, revealing what Chase told me a few days ago as I was falling asleep in his car. Over breakfast Chase told me how much he loved that spot on top of the hill, how every time he used to go there it gave him a moment of peace from the chaos of the city.

"I'm so happy for you Mon Mon".

I wish she could see the smile on my face right now, because I was feeling pretty god damn happy right now.

"Me too, drinks tonight, at dads?" I pace around my apartment as I wait for her reply.

"Don't ask silly questions, see you at 7".

The phone clicks as she ends the call. Not wanting my good mood to end, I connect my phone to my Bluetooth speaker and play one of my new favourite songs. Flinging open my wardrobe doors, I begin searching for outfits to take with me to Paris. The trip was in less than a week, and I was determined to look my best. Chase told me about the investors making an appearance at the show. Of course he played it off casually when I asked if he was worried but I could tell that he was. By the way his eyes shifted, by the way his jaw tensed.

I cross my legs as I take a seat at the edge of my bed and load up a clothing website. After a few minutes, I made an order for some very professional looking dresses and some definitely not professional dresses. The hours passed by, so I cooked a very sad looking microwave meal-for-one, sat at the table by myself and then took a very lonely shower. *I missed Chase's cooking. And his shower.*

I most definitely missed being in the shower with him. The thought of sneaking around with him on our trip gave me flashbacks to our trip to London. The hunger that he had in his eyes and the way he couldn't keep his hands off me during our dinner with our clients.

I knew he was out with Jordan and Noah tonight, and I really wanted to see my best friend. But I also really missed him. *Jesus, am I pouting right now?* From what I could see of my reflection in the steamy bathroom mirror, I was indeed pouting.

I chuckled at myself and began getting dressed.

The pub is busy as usual when I walk in and spot Rain waiting for me at the bar. She brings me in for a warm hug and I catch the smell of her perfume. We catch up with work gossip and she gives me the latest update on Skye and Steve.

"They've decided to go to couples therapy."

I spin the neck of my wine glass as she takes a sip from hers.

A slim hand appears in front of us, refilling our now empty glasses with more red wine.

My dad and Cathay are out on date night tonight, so Rosa, a local Spanish woman my dad met in the supermarket a few years ago, is manning the bar. My dad had asked her on a date once, she politely declined and told him that she played for the other team, they laughed about it and have been friends ever since.

"Oh, that's good" I reply, but judging by the way that Rain's shoulders hitch up I can tell that she doesn't agree but she hums anyway.

I give her the latest on me and Chase.

"Aren't you worried about what your team will say when they find out?", her voice is full of concern.

I breathe out a deep sigh.

"I was, at first, but now I think I'm so happy that I don't care." I shrug my shoulders at her. "Noah and Jordan already know anyway".

She breathes out, "well then," she clicks her glass against mine, "congratulations Mon."

We finish our bottle of wine and decide to head home when we both start slurring 'I love you' at each other, arms around each other as we stumble out of the pub. I'm glad that my dad isn't here tonight to catch us being so immature.

The week has flown by, and now I'm sitting in Chase's office the night before our flight to Paris. My eyes flick over the notes clutched in my hand, but my focus keeps drifting to him. He's across from me, speaking on the phone with Tom, his PR manager. I don't even notice how late it's getting until I glance around and see the corridor outside bathed in darkness, with no sounds from the other rooms.

Chase taps away on his laptop, his AirPods in, still deep in conversation. My gaze lingers on the veins running along his hands as his fingers glide across the keys. I bite my lip, breath catching when he shoots me a slow, teasing wink. The room feels charged, the voice on the other end of the call the only thing breaking the heavy silence. Then, without a word, Chase rises from his seat, his eyes dark with intention. He crosses the room with deliberate slowness, his gaze never leaving mine, and as he leans over me, the heat of his body brushes against mine.

He traces my jaw with his finger, the touch light but electrifying, sending a shiver down my spine.

His hand falls down my body, slowly tracing lower and lower until he tugs at the bottom of my skirt. I jump at his touch, as his thumb presses into my clit. A tingle shoots up my spine as I feel the dampness of my lace underwear against Chase's skin. I open my mouth to speak. But he places a finger from his left hand onto my lips.

"Don't make a sound," he warned. "This is an important call."

A whimper escapes my lips, as he tugs my underwear to the side and slips his middle finger inside me. My reaction is to moan but Chase just shakes his head as he continues his call. My chest rises as he adds another finger inside of me. From the slick sound it made, I was even wetter than I realised, damn near dripping for the man.

His eyes darken as continues talking, pumping his fingers back and forth. My legs begin to tremble and all I want to do is scream.

My breaths leave my mouth faster and faster, just as he pushes his thumb against my clit, a silent scream escapes. My heart is thumping erratically against my rib cage. His lips spread into a wide grin as he ends the call with a tap to his AirPods.

"Chase," I pull my skirt down and stand in front of him.

He tuts, "you did so well baby".

Chase sucks on his fingers before lowering his head to kiss the space below my ear. Pure evil. Part of me wants to call him a bastard for the way he tortured me, but I can't help but give into his touch. I just hope we get lots of alone time this weekend so I can get some payback on him.

Chase drops me off at my apartment to continue packing. After spending most of my nights this week staying with Chase, I miss coming home to my own space. A parcel bag awaits me as I turn the key in the door I bend down and swipe the bag into my arms. Heading to the kitchen I place the parcel onto my kitchen counter and remove the contents.

I add my new clothes to my black leather suitcase, zip it up and place it near the front door, with my hand luggage. I head back into the kitchen, my arms brushing past the roses in the vase, and make my way over to the sink. I fill up a small glass of water to feed my plant, which has blossomed into something beautiful. Small red flowers have grown from the centre. I give her a little pat as if to say 'well done'.

After a quick shower and change of clothes, I slip my laptop and notebook into my hand luggage. Reminding myself to go over the notes again on the plane. I really hope Be Creative wins this year. Right now, I want nothing more than for Chase to be happy. He deserves it. With the win, the investors will fully support the launch of his Australian office next year. I go to sleep that night dreaming of Chase winning the award and of finding him in his hotel room naked waiting for me to personally congratulate him.

•················•················•

I wake up early the next morning, slip into my office attire and head downstairs where Chase and the rest of the team are waiting in the limousine to take us to the airport.

He throws me a wink as I climb in and take a seat next to Noah. As much as I want to lean on Chase for the entire journey to the airport, it would be a smarter decision to sit next to Noah. *As long as he doesn't ask me about Skye.*

"Hey Monica, excited for Paris?" Noah asks as I clip in my seatbelt.

"I am, I've always wanted to visit Paris."

"You'll love it."

I give him a flat smile as I lean my sleepy head against the headrest.

"How's Skye by the way?".

God damn it Noah.

29 CHASE

Monica slips into the limousine and takes a seat next to Noah. It's killing me that she's so close I could touch her. She's wearing tight black trousers, chunky Mary Jane's and a white blouse that she's undone a few buttons on. The red lace from her bra peaks through as she bends over to place her phone into her bag causing my cock to swell a little, suddenly I'm very glad for the laptop sitting on my lap.

I'm glad Monica is here, as well as the whole team, but having her by my side for the award show soothes my anxiety. We've all got a big night ahead of us, but we'll be in Paris early enough to check into the hotel and wind down before the show.

My room is on the same floor as hers, Noah's, Jake's and Chelsea's. The rest of the team are on the third floor. I just hope Noah bought his earplugs, since his room is in the middle of mine and Monica's.

We make it through the busy airport, past the painfully slow security and into first class on the plane without any issues.

Using the next hour or so of this journey to catch up on some sleep, I shut my eyes and dream of all the things I'm going to do to Monica in Paris.

I'm shaken awake by Noah nudging my shoulder, letting me know that we've landed. There's a chill in the air as we step outside of the Charles de Gaulle airport to wait for our hotel minibus transfer.

Jake heads to the hotel reception desk as we walk in, taking the lead on checking us all in. The team disperses to use the bathrooms and look around the hotel lobby. There's a small quaint library to the left of me and a bar and lounge to the right of me. I have a feeling that the bar has a glass of whiskey with my name on it.

I pull out my phone and begin scrolling through the mass amount of emails that have already started to build up. My jaw tenses a little as a call from Jordan pops up on my phone but I ignore it. I'm not in the mood for his wind ups right now. I need to be in the best mindset for tonight, I can't have anything go wrong.

A rapid tap on my shoulder draws my attention from my phone and I turn.

"When I call you, fucking answer your phone" Jordan barks as he brings me in for a hug.

"Jordan, what are you doing here?".

"Couldn't miss my baby bro winning another award now, could I?".

A chuckle escapes me as I step back from Jordan. I think I was wrong, having him here could help me relax a little. He is my drinking partner after all.

"Glad you could make it bro," I tell him as I watch Monica walk out of the library, chatting away with Chelsea.

Jordan shoves his hands into pockets and shifts his gaze to where I'm staring.

"Boy, I feel sorry for whoever is sleeping next to your room".

"Shut up Jordan".

Jake strides over and hands us our keycards. Jordan tells me his room is a few doors down from mine, and I agree to meet him downstairs for some pre-drinks before tonight's ceremony.

The award venue is a short drive from our hotel, which I'm glad about. I've had long journeys to award shows in the past and all it does is allow me more time for my anxiety to increase.

I take in three deep breaths as I enter my room and place my suitcase onto the desk. After waiting a few minutes, I pop my head out the door to look down the corridor and see everyone has entered their rooms.

My fingers tap across the screen and within a few seconds, there's a light knock at my door. Her black wavy hair wraps around my hand, as I pull Monica into me and crash my lips onto hers, kicking the door closed behind her. A deep groan rumbles in my throat as I kiss her jaw.

"Not being able to touch you when you're so close is driving me crazy".

"How crazy Mr Marino?"
she tips her head to the side, giving me full access to her neck. My tongue flicks over her ear causing a deep breath to escape her lips. My hand flies to unbuckle my belt as I push Monica onto her knees. Her eyelashes flutter as she smirks, pulling down my trousers. Her hair snakes around my wrist as I use the other hand to pull down my boxers. She leans forward on her hands, staring up at me with her mouth open. Her wet tongue flies out as I place the head of my cock onto her bottom lip and thrust forward.

My hands form into fists at how loud I want to scream her name. She pulls me out of her mouth for a second, placing her finger onto her lips and telling me to be quiet. She's getting payback on me for last night. *That's my girl.*

I smile down at her as she wraps her hands around my cock and places it back into her mouth. Monica looks like a goddamn sex goddess on her knees, bobbing her head back and forth. A tingle shoots up my spine as I continue bucking my hips until her mouth fills with my come.

I zip my trousers up and bring Monica back onto her feet. She places a kiss on my cheek before slipping out of the door and returning back to her room. Pulling my phone from my pocket, I fired off a text message to Jordan telling him to meet me downstairs at the bar in an hour.

My heart tugs at the memory of how only a few months ago Monica and I sat around a bar table in a hotel drinking, as strangers.

Not knowing that she would enter my life and cause an absolute storm. That's when the thought hits me, I would do anything to make sure she stays in my life. Like, have a conversation with my brother about a certain deal.

After a shower, change of clothes and a last minute proof read of my speech, I leave my room to head downstairs. I slip a note under Monica's door and tell her to meet me at the bar. We still have a few hours before the show, plenty of time to knock back a few shots.

I slide into a booth where Jordan is sitting and watch Monica's face light up as she walks in and spots my brother next to me.

They both hug and I slide onto the opposite side, throwing my arm over her and she sits next to me. I watch her smile as she catches up with Jordan, telling him about Rain's kitten and our plans to go ice skating tomorrow.

Monica clears her throat.

"Shots anyone?"

We both hum in agreement and she slips out of the booth and heads to the bar.

Once Monica is out of earshot, I lean over the table and clear my throat. Now that I have a moment I turn my attention to Jordan.

"Brother, we need to talk".

A groan escapes his mouth, and I have a feeling he knows exactly what I'm going to say.

30 MONICA

The first half of the trip was a mix of both torturous and rewarding moments. Not being able to cuddle up to Chase on the plane or kiss him every time he flashed me a wink was tough, but it was worth it to get a little payback for what happened last night. After leaving Chase's room, I went over my notes for the evening with Jake, brewed myself a strong coffee, and slipped into the crimson red velvet dress I'd picked out specifically for the show.

While packing the night before, I noticed the zip on my 'lucky' silver dress had broken.

I immediately called Rain, who reassured me it wasn't an omen or anything to worry about – just my overactive paranoia. I folded the dress, tucked it back into the wardrobe, and promised myself I'd have it fixed once I got back from Paris.

As I finished applying my makeup, my thoughts drifted to tonight's show – the live band, the endless cocktails, and the meal that would set the tone for the evening. My stomach rumbled at the thought of the French cuisine tasting experience waiting for me. I *really* needed to stop skipping breakfast.

I've always loved travelling, especially the thrill of sampling new foods, and tonight, I couldn't wait to indulge. One of my fondest memories is when my father took me to my abuela's house in Valencia during the summer break. We spent hours in her bustling kitchen, chopping and prepping ingredients to make her famous paella. The radio played lively Spanish songs, and we couldn't help but dance around, caught up in the joy of the moment. Before we left that summer, I hugged her tightly, unwilling to let go. There was something about three generations of our family sharing those precious moments together that made me realise I'd want a family of my own one day—with someone who loved me as deeply as I loved them.

I couldn't help but fantasise about the possibility of Chase and I travelling together. Sunbathing on a beach somewhere, or skiing in the mountains. Still, I tried not to get too carried away when I thought about a future with him.

As much as sneaking around the office is exciting, I couldn't ignore the reality of what might happen when everyone eventually finds out.

What if he offers me a business partnership one day, and in return, I become the target of office disdain?

What if, one day, he breaks my heart, and I'm forced to walk away from the best job I've ever had and the team that feels like family?

All this heavy thinking has me feeling stressed, so I open the box of complementary luxury treats next to the coffee machine and nibble on one of the white and dark chocolates. The sugar causes my mouth to salivate, and I moan at how good it tastes. A piece of paper rustling under my door draws my attention away from the flavour explosion in my mouth.

A wide smile appears on my face as I read a note from Chase asking me to meet him downstairs. I finish applying my makeup with a quick swipe of my red lipstick and place it inside my purse. I take a seat at the leather armchair and tie up the string on my silver strappy high heels around my legs. I stand to grab my purse, jacket and keycard and head downstairs to meet Chase.

My heels click against the marbled floor of the hotel lobby as I exit the lift and head towards the bar. As I walk in I take a second to appreciate the gold and white decor. There's a chandelier hanging above the wooden bar, lines of booths and tables and low music plays across the room. I round the corner and spot a familiar face.

Jordan brings me into a hug, and I slide next to Chase in the booth. We both catch up a little as I blabber on about Rain's new kitten. When all I want to do is turn to Chase and tell him how fucking sexy, he looks wearing that tux. *And how I want him in my hotel bed wearing nothing but that bow tie.*

"Shots anyone?". I blurt out because right now I'm going to need something strong to get me through a night of fighting the urge to launch myself at Chase.

There's a queue of people waiting to be served so I turn and lean against the bar, looking back over at the booth where we're sitting. Chase is pointing his finger at himself and then at me. I tip my head to the side in confusion.

After a few minutes a bartender walks over to me, and I ask for three shots of vodka. As I juggle two shots in one hand I walk back over to the booth where Chase and Jordan are having a heated conversation.

As I get closer, Chase raises his voice and snaps.

"The deal is fucking off".

Trying to break the tension between them, I place each shot in front of us. Neither of them flinches to reach the small glasses of spirit.

"What deal are you talking about?". My voice is full of concern, as I watch them engage in a staring match.

"Jordan. Don't." Chase's jaw ticks.

What the fuck is happening?

"Fuck you, Chase."

Anger bubbles up inside me. How dare Jordan talk to his brother like that? I furrow my eyebrows at Jordan, and I open my mouth to speak, but he continues talking.

"We had an agreement. The deal was simple. I don't settle until he does, and now my brother's gone and broken it. Are you happy, Monica? This is what I get for trusting him."

Jordan slams his hand down onto the table, slips out of the booth and storms off.

I stare at Chase for a moment trying to process what just happened. I thought we had something real. But now I'm wondering if I was just part of some game he was playing with his brother. How could he not tell me? What does this mean for us?

I take one of the shots of Vodka and down it. My hand begins to shake as I place the glass back onto the table.

"Monica, let me explain."

I stand and slip into the seat opposite him, to see his face.

"Was I just a way for you to get out of some stupid deal?" I snake my hand around Jordan's untouched shot and down it. The alcohol burns, but it's nothing compared to the fire raging inside me.

"Monica, I get why you're angry. I should've told you sooner. The deal with Jordan—it started as a joke, a stupid promise between brothers when neither of us wanted to settle down. But it's been weighing on me for a while now."

My eyes sting, tears threatening to spill. "You didn't trust me enough to tell me about this? What else are you hiding, Chase?"

"Nothing. I'm not hiding anything." His voice rises slightly, and I see the flash of frustration in his eyes. Like he has the right to be mad.

I grab his shot, my hands trembling. I put it down, slamming the glass on the table. "Do you even love me, Chase? Or is this just about proving a point to Jordan?"

His face softens, and for a moment, I see the man I thought I knew.

"Of course I love you." He takes a deep breath out. "I told Jordan I'm done, Monica. The deal meant nothing the moment I met you. I didn't need to prove anything to him—I just needed you."

I shake my head. His words feel hollow, like an echo of something I want to believe but can't.

"You're still living by his rules, not your own—or ours." A tear slips free, and I swipe at it angrily.

"Please, Mia Cara." His voice is almost a whisper. "I hate it when you cry." He reaches for my hand, but I pull away.

"It's too much, Chase. Too much."

I stand on shaky legs, the weight of his confession crashing down on me. When I try to leave, his hand closes around my wrist. My anger erupts like a storm. My chest tightens, my breaths coming shallow as his hand closes around my wrist. For a moment, I think I might scream. Instead, I channel every ounce of rage into my voice.

"Don't. You. Dare."

"Cherry…".

His voice is so quiet now.

"I thought you were different. I thought we were real."

He lets go immediately, pain flashing across his face. But I don't care. I throw my hand over my mouth to stifle the sob rising in my throat and bolt for the door, leaving him—and everything we had—behind.

31 CHASE

Her small hand slips from my grip, and I watch the only woman I've ever loved bolt for the door. She runs—like being near me another second will destroy her completely. My chest tightens, the burn spreading like wildfire. What have I done?

No. What have we done?

Fucking Jordan. He started this mess, showing up in Paris uninvited, stirring shit like it was his job, and then walking away the second the flames got too hot. He threw the match, sure—but I'm the one who let it burn out of control.

I want to hate him, but the truth is, I can't pin this all on Jordan.

This mess? It's on me. My cowardice. My inability to own up to my mistakes until it was too late.

And now she's gone.

In less than an hour, I could be standing on stage accepting an award, but that means nothing if she's not in the crowd. How am I supposed to care about applause that doesn't come from her? About cameras that don't capture her smile?

I can already see her in my mind, the way her hands would clap together—small, delicate, perfect. Her lips curving into that radiant, effortless smile that lights up the whole damn room.

But she won't be there.

And for the first time in my life, I don't feel like a winner.

I head out of the bar a minute or so after she leaves. My head spins from left to right, from the door to the reception, from the library to the toilets. If she thinks I won't enter the women's bathroom and drag her out here so I can make things right, then she's very wrong.

My feet begin walking towards the bathrooms, when Chelsea exits the door, she's startled as I stand there with my hands behind my head.

"Everything okay boss?", she furrowed her eyebrows at me.

"Chelsea is Monica in there?". She shrugs before heading back inside, calls her name and then returns to me shaking her head.

Damn it. I give her a flat face smile before making my way to the lifts. My foot taps rapidly on the tiled floor as I wait. The doors fly open, and I enter. I stare in disgust at my reflection in the mirror. How could I have done this to her?

The lift doors ping open on our floor, and I race to her room. I knock twice before banging my fist against it. Noah opens his door and looks around to see what the noise is.

"Dude, where's the fire?", he continued buttoning up his white shirt.

"Where's Monica?" I spit.

"She knocked on my door a few minutes ago and gave me her keycard".

"Why would she do that?"

"I guessed she gave it to me because she was staying with you tonight. I thought she was hinting for me to stay in her room so I wouldn't hear you guys…erm…after the award show" he smirks and wiggles his eyebrows.

"Give me her card".

He steps inside, then comes back with her card in his hand. I grab it from him and walk into her room. Her perfume still lingers, but as I look around, it hits me—there's nothing here. No clothes, no suitcase, no sign of her. She's gone. All of it.

My breath catches in my chest, and my heart shatters. My phone buzzes in my pocket, and I pull it out to see the reminder—transport for the award show in thirty minutes. I can't go without her.

The team can go without me. I don't care if it sounds crazy. How the hell am I supposed to stand in front of my investors or my team and read that bullshit speech about loyalty and teamwork when she's just disappeared on me? I sit down on her bed, staring at my hands, trying to process it. And then I can't take it anymore. I bury my face in my hands and scream.

"Err… everything alright, boss?"

I'd completely forgotten Noah was still behind me when I walked into her room. The floodgates open. I'm sure Noah already knows a small amount about Monica and me. But I tell him everything anyway — about Monica, about the stupid deal with Jordan, and how I've fallen so hard for her it physically hurts. Every word spills out in a rush, my voice breaking under the weight of it all.

Noah exhales, crossing his arms as he leans against the doorframe, watching me unravel.

"Alright, here's what you're going to do, Chase. Go to the award show, win that damn trophy we've all busted our asses for, charm the investors, have a good evening—and let her cool off."

I lift my head from my hands, squinting at him like he's lost his mind.

"She needs space right now," he says firmly. "If you push her, you'll only make it worse. I'll tell the team that Monica had a family emergency and had to go home".

He's right, but there's no way I'm telling him that. I straighten up, tug at the lapels of my black Armani tux, and smooth down the front. The hallway outside is busy with muffled sounds—doors closing, the faint ding of a lift, and the quiet hum of people moving about. The air smells like hotel-cleaner and whatever floral scent they pump through the vents to make the place feel expensive.

I head over to Noah, give him a hard pat on the shoulder, and slip out the door without saying anything else. As I walk down the soft, carpeted corridor, I grab my phone and call her. She doesn't answer so I type out a quick message.

Me:

Call me.

Me:

Please

Me:

I need to explain

Me:

I love you

Then I shove the phone back in my pocket, half-wishing it would buzz instantly.

Twenty minutes later, the whole team is in the lobby, gathered near the massive glass doors where the limousine is parked outside, all shiny and perfect under the hotel's spotlights. Everyone's here, dressed sharp, buzzing with excitement—except for the one person I need by my side.

I pull out my phone and try her number again. For the hundredth, maybe thousandth time. Still nothing. Still no answer.

Jordan walks over, his shoes making soft clicks on the marble floor. He stops next to me, looking like he's carrying the weight of the world on his face, the kind of look that says he knows exactly how screwed I feel right now.

"I'm sorry, Chase, but I was pissed."

"Jordan, you're forgiven—if you can help me find Monica." I shove my phone at him, the screen lighting up with dozens of unanswered texts and calls.

"Did you ask reception?"

I freeze, then shake my head. Of course I didn't think of that. My brain's been a mess since I walked into her empty room.

Jordan doesn't waste a second. He heads straight to the hotel receptionist while I stand there, my pulse hammering.

He's got his back to me, but when he turns around, his head is low, and his steps are slow. That look on his face—it's one I've never seen before. It's heartbreak, clear as day. And that can only mean bad news.

"The hotel called her a taxi about half an hour ago," he says quietly.

My jaw tightens, teeth grinding as I shake my head in frustration.

"She's at the airport, Chase," Jordan adds, his voice softer this time.

I glance down at my Rolex, my mind racing. Do I have enough time to get to the airport, drag her back where she belongs, and still make it to the award show?

Jordan watches me, reading my expression like a book. "Whatever you're thinking, you can't miss that award show."

"With all due respect, brother, I'm done listening to you," I snap, my voice sharp.

He groans, rolling his eyes, before stepping aside to stand next to Noah. I'm not worried about falling out with Jordan. God knows we've had worse fall outs. A year ago, Jordan bet ten grand on a horse at the Grand Nationals, a horse I told him not to bet on, and he lost all his money. One thing led to another, and I walked out of the Nationals with a black eye and Jordan with a split lip.

The team's energy shifts as they start cheering, filing out through the main glass doors to the sleek black limo waiting out front. Their excitement feels like a slap in the face.

Meanwhile, my feet refuse to move. Do I stick with the plan or go after her? I'm torn, drowning in indecision, when my phone buzzes in my pocket.

Cherry:

Stop calling me.

Cherry:

We'll talk on Monday.

Her words hit me like a punch to the gut. Monday? How the hell am I supposed to wait until Monday?

My heart hammers inside my chest, each beat echoing with nerves and regret. The short text message from her gives me a sliver of hope—a lifeline, really—that I'll get the chance to tell her how sorry I am for all of this. But not now. For now, I must give her space.

The evening air bites against my skin as I step outside, sharp and unforgiving, much like the knot twisting in my stomach. I climb into the limousine last, hesitating just long enough to second-guess myself. Am I doing the right thing?

My team doesn't seem to share my inner turmoil. They're all laughter and cheers, clinking champagne glasses like this is the best night of their lives. I can't bring myself to join them. Instead, I sit stiffly, staring straight ahead, trapped in my own silence, letting their celebration swirl around me.

The ride feels endless, but eventually, we pull up to the venue. The bright flashes of cameras and the murmur of journalists waiting outside pull me out of my daze. And that's when it hits me—like a punch to the gut.

Monica has my speech.

My chest tightens, and then a maniacal laugh bursts out of me, startling even myself. Of course, she has it. Of course, I'm going to end up on stage in front of everyone with nothing to say. It's almost poetic, really. A public reckoning for everything I've put her through. For once, I'm not even mad. If anything, I'm proud. She knew exactly what she was doing.

The laugh fades, but a faint smile lingers on my face as I step out of the limousine. The cameras flash, and the crowd buzzes with energy, but I don't care about any of it. I walk inside, my team trailing behind me, oblivious to the chaos brewing inside my head. Tonight, I'll stand on that stage like a fool with no notes to hide behind, and honestly?

It feels like justice.

32 MONICA

He's smiling. Smiling and laughing for the cameras like nothing happened. Like he didn't tear my heart into a million pieces. I flick through the photos on my phone, each one pissing me off more than the last. Sitting in the sterile airport terminal, I feel the hum of the overhead announcements, repeating in French, then again, in English.

He won't be smiling when he finds out I have his speech.

I take a deep breath, forcing myself to focus. In a few hours, I'll be back home. With Carlos, Rain, Skye. People who give a damn about me.

People who say they love me because they mean it—not to prove some dumb point. My chest tightens as my eyes sting, burning behind my eyelids. Don't cry. Don't cry.

I'm grateful I hadn't unpacked my suitcase, except for the evening dress I'm still wearing, which made for a quick exit. I stormed to my room, grabbed my things, handed Noah my keycard, and asked the hotel to call a taxi to the airport. My plan had been to sneak into his room after the award show and stay the night, but I moved on autopilot. All I could think about was getting away from him.

Him.

Chase.

I can't even say his name in my head without my heart twisting. A single tear slips down my cheek, betraying me. An elderly woman sitting next to me notices and hands me a tissue. She doesn't say a word, just watches as I try to keep it together. I don't know what language she speaks, but I thank her anyway, my voice trembling. My nose sniffles and I place the tissue back into my jacket pocket. I have a feeling I'm going to need it again tonight.

While I wait, I connect to the airport's free Wi-Fi and quickly send a text to Rain.

Me:

Change of plan.

Me:

I'm coming home.

Rain (Bestie):

OMG, what happened?

Rain (Bestie):

If Chase did something, I'm poking him in the eye!

Rain (Bestie):

Doesn't matter how tall you are, a poke in the eye still hurts!

Me:

Love you. See you soon.

A small smile tugs at my lips. Rain always knows how to make me laugh, even when she has no idea I need it.

An hour later, a flight attendant approaches the check-in counter. I take a shaky breath, my heart hammering in my chest, and hand her my passport. Maybe the simple act of leaving will help ease the ache gnawing at me.

But it doesn't. Leaving makes me feel guilty—like I'm running away when things got tough. Am I just like my mother? Most girls dream of being just like their mothers—strong, confident, sure of themselves. I'm doing everything I can not to be like mine. I used to think I'd be different. I would do anything not to be like her. My mother was a quitter. And now... I wonder if I am, too. Things got complicated, and I just walked away.

I promised myself I'd never be that person.

Yet here I am, taking the easy way out, just like she did.

God, I am like her. The thought stings more than I expected. I hate that I'm repeating her mistakes, hating myself for it. But then... how much Chase hurt me, how he shattered everything we had, it's still fresh, raw.

The pain outweighs everything else, but is that enough to justify running? To justify being a coward?

My mind circles, too tired to stop, and the weight of it all presses on my temples. I wish I could just shut it off.

I can hear Skye's voice in the back of my mind telling me 'I told you so'. I hope she won't be too mad when I tell her what happened. I should have listened to her when she tried to warn me. I guess I learned my lesson the hard way.

I stuff my small suitcase into the overhead compartment and tuck my hand luggage under the seat in front of me. The flight attendant begins the safety demonstration, but my mind drifts. The weight of the day's events makes my eyelids grow heavy. As soon as I feel the plane's wheels lift off the runway, I close my eyes and let sleep take over.

•················•················•

The flight and the journey back to Dad's pub blur together. Rain surprised me at Manchester Airport.

After I sent her that text, she made her way straight to my dad's pub and demanded he meet me at the arrivals hall with her.

As I dragged my noisy suitcase through the terminal and out the doors, I spotted tiny Rain, holding sunflowers in her hands, standing beside my dad. She wrapped me in a tight hug, and my dad kissed the top of my head, a soft, comforting gesture.

"Come on, mi amor, let's get you home."

"Thanks, Dad."

He threw his arm around me, and we headed toward the multi-story car park. A short while later we all sat around a booth at The Dog and Gun. The pub was full of its usual patriots on a Saturday night. Sounds of glasses clicking, people chatting and a slightly drunk couple singing on the karaoke filled the atmosphere.

As much as I was relieved to be home, all I wanted was to be with Chase and the rest of the team. I'd been looking forward to the trip for so long—and so had Chase. How could everything go so wrong in such a short time? I didn't even notice the tears until Rain gently ran her hand down my back.

"Mon, tell us what happened?"

I exhaled sharply, feeling the weight of everything.

"I think I'll give you some space, mi amor. If you need me, you know where I'll be."

I gave my dad a teary smile as he walked back to the bar where Cathay was serving customers. This was why I loved him so much—he always knew when to step in and when to give me room.

I told Rain everything, and after a few long moments of silence, she finally spoke.

"That bastard! I'll kill them both."

A soft laugh escaped my lips.

"Please don't. The prison's parking is awful."

She smiled, reaching over to squeeze my hand.

"How long before Skye gives me the 'I told you so' speech?"

I dabbed at the corners of my eyes with the tissue I'd kept in my pocket earlier. It was now stained with mascara smudges, and I tossed it onto the table as Rain handed me a fresh napkin.

"I don't know, but I do know she'll be there for you, no matter what."

Skye always was. She was the older sister everyone needed. Even though she was only three years older than Rain and me, she felt more like a mother figure than anything else.

An hour later, Skye walked into the busy pub and joined us at the table. I could really go for a glass of white wine, but I knew it would just make my headache worse.

We all agreed on chamomile tea instead, as Rain had suggested it for its calming properties. It tasted like perfume, but it did soothe my nerves.

I filled Skye in on everything, and I was grateful she'd be the last person I'd have to repeat this to. Saying it one more time might've turned my headache into a full-blown migraine.

She pulled a similar expression to her sister before leaning forward to rub slow circles with her thumb on my hand.

"I'm so sorry that happened Mon, but—".

Oh god, here we go.

"You're one of the strongest people I know. If anyone is going to come out better on the other side, it'll be you."

Oh.

"Thanks Skye. Love you both."

"Love you too", they both said at the same time.

"Oh, and I told you so."

Ah, there we go.

Skye begins her speech and doesn't end until we empty the bottle of wine.

•..................•..................•

It had been a few hours since arriving back in Manchester, Skye and Rain had gone home and dad had shut the pub up for the night.

"Can I get you anything, love?" Cathay asked me as she threw a blanket over me.

"No, thank you. I'm good." I wiggled my toes against the fluffy fabric as I lay on the soft sofa. My dad lived above the pub, so it made sense staying here tonight. Going back to my apartment and seeing Chase's stuff there would hurt too much right now. Since my dad had turned my old room into an office, I opted for sleeping on the sofa.

"If you need me, I'll be in the other room burying my head in a good thriller book".

Cathay waved goodbye to me as she left the room. My dad is sitting in the armchair next to me, with a very sombre expression on his face.

"I'll be fine dad; I just need some sleep". "I worry for you. I want you to be happy. You don't need to tell me what happened, but I want you to know that if you need me, I'm here for you. te amo"

"Te amo dad"

He gives me a bright smile before leaving to join Cathay in the other room.

I go to sleep dreaming of ice skating on the Eiffel Tower, like I have so many nights these past few weeks, except this time when I look around, I'm all alone.

33 CHASE

I won.

We won.

Be Creative walked away with the Best Marketing Agency award for the fifth year in a row.

I should be celebrating, I should be grateful, happy.

I feel nothing. The host stands on stage announcing the rest of the awards. A person from each company attending goes up to collect their trophy and return to their tables. The tables have been decorated with white tablecloths, golden coloured candles, named place cards and small metal replicas of the Eiffel Tower. The memory of me promising Monica to take her ice skating has my chest aching.

"Boss?".

I bring myself back to reality and realise Noah is talking to me.

"You need to go up. Go get your award."

But my legs don't move. Do I go up there with no speech prepared and stand there like a fool? Should I cop out and send Noah instead of me?

"I can't." I whisper to him.

"Chase, get up there. Don't let us down now. Don't be a coward".

Any other night and I would have punched him in the nose for calling me that. But he is right.

He pats me twice on the shoulder before I stand to make my way over to the stage. A round of applause fills the room.

I pass the host as she hands me the glass trophy. Her blonde waves fall down her shoulders, down her green silky dress. She throws me a wink and I almost feel insulted.

I greet the crowd in French and begin my unprepared speech.

For the next fifteen minutes I ramble on about the importance of teamwork, honesty and loyalty in the workplace and amongst a team. But the entire time all I can think about is Monica.

How I'm looking out at the crowd wishing she was there smiling back at me.

Liar.

Spineless.

Traitor.

That little voice in my head pops up again.

I need a fucking drink.

I thank the award show, the crowd, the chefs for the meal they prepared and served, the live band and finally my team. I raise the award above my head as I walk off stage back over to my team. With the award show over, the live band has been replaced by a DJ booth. The venue lights have been dimmed, and the crowd floods the dance floor as French rap music booms through the speakers.

The team and the crowd make their way over to the dancefloor, as I head over to the bar. I order myself a glass of whiskey and tell the bartender to leave the bottle next to my empty glass.

Noah strides up and takes the empty stool next to me. I gesture to the bartender to bring us another glass.

Noah fills his own glass and clicks it against mine. He congratulates me and I remind him that the team deserves all the credit. Yes, I bring in the clients but they're the ones who have put in the hard work and long hours.

The thought of late nights in the office has me remembering when I'd stay late at my desk to finish off signing contracts. She'd bring me dinner and keep me company. She kept me sane.

The saying is true; you really don't know what you've got until its gone. I bow my head slightly, feeling sorry for myself. The room is filled with people enjoying their night, drinking, laughing, singing. But that all blurs around me, I can only focus on one thing.

My grip tightens around the glass in my hand.

"Great job on the speech boss. The team are having a great time. It's not the same without Monica though".

You can say that again.

I swipe the bottle from next to me.

"Enjoy your night, Noah."

Whiskey in hand, I make my way to the venue's garden. Small fairy lights cover the archway to the water fountain as I walk through the greenery. I take a seat at the rounded stone foundation and scroll through the photos of me and Monica on my phone.

The last one I took of her; she was wrapped up in my bed sheets on a lazy Sunday morning. Her long-bronzed legs hugged the white fabric as I snuck out of bed to make coffee for us as she slept.

I place my phone back into my jacket pocket and take a swig on the bottle. The amber liquid burns in my throat but it doesn't burn as much as my chest does.

A dark figure appears next to me, even though my vision begins to haze from the alcohol, I would recognise my brother anywhere.

"Hey bro."

"Hey Jord."

"She'll forgive you."

I let out a deep sigh.

"I really hope so. I fucking love her."

He claps my shoulder with his hand as he swipes the bottle from me.

"I know you do."

"I am sorry for what happened Chase. Think it's time for me to fucking grow up".

I turn my head towards him to look him in the eyes. I could always tell when my brother is lying, his left eye usually twitches a little. This time, nothing.

"Cheers to that brother".

He takes a swig of whiskey from the bottle before passing it back over to me. We finish the bottle between us and head back inside to join the team in celebration.

•················•·················•

The next morning our transport arrives early to take us to the airport. The next few hours blur together as we pack, leave the hotel and head back to the airport to catch our return flight to Manchester. I cancelled the ice-skating trip and told the team that we'd run out of time. I know it's unfair to the team and I'll make it up to them, but I couldn't do it. Not without her.

From the minute we land my phone is flooded with congratulation messages, emails from my investors and text messages from Tom. With the win, our investors will fully financially support the launch of the Australian office next year.

We all make our way back to our own apartments and homes on Sunday morning. The day passes by quickly as I keep myself distracted. I hit the gym, refuel my car, restock my fridge, and place an order online for a dozen red roses to be sent to Monica's apartment.

I take a hot shower, watching as the steam fills the room. Monica's products are still standing in my shower. I open the shampoo and take a deep inhale. Wondering when I became the creep that sniffs a girl's shampoo from the bottle.

I chuckle at myself as I wrap the soft cotton towel around my waist and enter my bedroom.

The scenarios of what could happen tomorrow play through my mind. Either way, I'm going to make it clear to her that she's the girl I love, she's the one that I want to laugh, joke and cry with, she's the girl I want to spend the rest of my life with.

Woah.

My eyes flick to my wooden chest of drawers as I walk over and pull open the top drawer. I search through my ties and bow ties and find the small black velvet box I was looking for.

My grandmother's diamond ring sparkles under the light as I stare down at it. I place it into the inside pocket of my leather satchel.

I toss and turn all night as my mind deprives my body of sleep. I switch between working out, to watching TV, to sending emails until the sun rises.

Monday morning arrives so I start my week how I start every week. I shower, get dressed, make a double espresso to go, enter my BMW and head to the office.

I double checked the inside pocket of my satchel to make sure the small box I placed in there the night before, didn't grow legs and walk away. Content that the box is safely in the building with me, I head to my office.

It's early enough that the team hasn't arrived yet. I pace around my office until the lift doors ping and the sounds of heels clicking along the floor fill the corridor.

I face the window, looking at the city skyline as she enters my office.

"Hi Chase."

My shoulders instantly relax at the sound of her voice. A smile spreads across my face as I turn to face Monica.

But my smile drops as I notice she's holding an empty cardboard box.

No.

"This was never going to work, Chase. One of us was bound to get hurt".
She winces at the last word.

"I think this is what's best for me. And you."

If I could just open my goddamn mouth and speak. But I can't find the words.

She spins on her heels as she heads to her own office and begins to pack the contents of her desk into the empty box. I'm so tempted to grab the box from her hands and empty her belongings onto the desk in my office.

She places her laptop from her bag slowly onto the desk and leaves a white envelope on top.

The next few minutes blur as she tapes up the cardboard box and makes her way back down the corridor towards the lift. My hand reaches out behind her. I need to stop her and tell her how sorry I am. How I've changed so much over the last few months. For the better.

She makes me want to be better.

She pushes the call button and waits to face the lift doors. I reach my hand out to touch her, but it's like she's made of glass. If I touch her I might break her even more.

"Monica, I'm sorry."

She turns slowly to face me, her eyes slightly glassy. The lift clunks as it stops on our floor and pings as the doors slide open.

"Me too Chase".

The words leave her mouth softly.

Why on earth would she need to apologise?

"I quit".

34 MONICA

As soon as the lift door shuts, I burst into tears. The sobs escape my body faster than I can stop them. The box wobbles in my hand as I exit the lift and walk across the lobby. I passed some members of the team on my way out. I wish I had the chance to say goodbye to them and thank them for the last few months.

Instead, I keep my head down as I make my way back to my car. I haven't decided what I'm going to do with my car yet. That's a thought for later.

My handshakes as I open the car door and place the taped-up box in the back seats. I have so many thoughts running through my mind right now, I'm scrambling to organise them

The memory of Chase's heartbroken face is one that haunts me.

Last night I went back to my apartment. I unpacked my unworn clothes and placed them back into my wardrobe. I took one look at my favourite silver dress and a fit of rage took over. The dress is currently sitting in my bathroom bin cut into tiny little pieces.

I don't want any memories of him. I packed all his stuff that he left at mine, his toothbrush, spare shirts, aftershave, into a box and mailed it to his home address.

I told myself last night I was done with him. But am I really? I kept the dried-up petals from all the roses he bought me in a small box. I kept all the receipts from our dinner dates. I kept all the sticky notes he'd leave at my desk.

A groan leaves my body as I pull into the car park of my apartment. I might be jobless, but I have enough in my savings to keep me afloat for a few months at least.

I could always go back to working at my dad's pub.

I drop my keys onto the cold kitchen counter as I enter my quiet apartment. For the first time in my adult life, I have nowhere to be.

So, I start with the one place I know my favourite people will be waiting for me. As the evening creeps up, I take a hot shower and slip into some warm winter clothes.

I wrap the fluffy cream scarf that I purchased at the Manchester Christmas market last year, around my neck before I head out of the door. My feet stop in place as I look at the coat rack next to the door and realise my white leather jacket is missing.

Dammit.

I must have left it at Chase's apartment. I can't cut ties with two of my favourite items of clothing in the same week, I'm just asking for a mental breakdown, but I also can't deal with seeing Chase so soon to ask him for my stuff back. I decided to wear a different jacket and remind myself to send him a text message asking for the jacket and the rest of my stuff back.

As I walk outside into the brisk evening air, I order myself an Uber to The Dog and Gun. Within a few minutes I walked inside and find Rain sitting at the bar watching my dad pour a glass of wine for us both.

She pulls me into a tight hug I so desperately needed. She already knows about today's events as I called her last night to ensure I was doing the right thing. She responded with 'Duh'.

We agreed not to speak about him for the rest of the evening. I made an inner promise not to think about him for the rest of the evening.

So, I don't. I don't think about him for the rest of the week.

Or the rest of the month.

A few weeks ago by since I quit my job at Be Creative and I filled my time with working shifts at the pub alongside dad and Cathay.

Cathay would work shorter day shifts at her cafe and then join my dad in the evening. The three of us had a good dynamic going.

It's moderately busy for a Friday night. As winter creeps up on us, the pub tends to see less and less patriots, but the usuals always swing by for a pint or two.

One of our regulars is chatting away in front of me as I pull a pint of beer for him. My eyes begin to burn as I realise just how tired I am. I can't imagine how bad the bags are under my eyes.

I've barely slept the last few weeks; every night I toss and turn until the sun comes booming through my bedroom window. I fake a smile and nod as the man standing in front of me continues his one-way conversation about politics.

My dad and Cathay are stocking the mini fridge with soft drinks next to me, but they stop their conversation as the pub doors swing open.

He strides slowly up to the bar, my white leather jacket clutched tightly in his hands.

My heart pounds, my palms slick with sweat. As I pass a pint glass to the customer in front of me, it almost slips through my fingers. I watch as the customer returns to his table, wishing he wouldn't. Wishing he'd stay and order a dozen more drinks—anything to keep me from having to face Chase.

But there's no escaping it. I straighten my spine, take a steadying breath, and meet his gaze.

"Hi".

"Hi". Chase responds softly.

"You cut your hair. It looks nice," he says.

I resist the urge to fidget but I run my hand through my freshly cut bob.

"Decided to switch things up," I reply, keeping my tone casual. "What are you doing here, Chase?"

He lifts my jacket slightly, holding it out as if that's answer enough. "You left this at mine."

I decided in the end not to reach out and ask for my stuff back. As much as it was heartbreaking to part ways with my favourite white leather jacket, material items could be replaced. Which Rain and Skye did, with some extra decor added.

Reaching out, I take it from him, and for the briefest moment, my fingers brush his. The contact sends a spark across my skin, but I shake it off. Static. That's all it is. It's not him—I don't feel anything for him anymore. At least, that's what I tell myself.

Liar.

Shut up.

"Thank you." My smile is flat, devoid of warmth. It's all Chase deserves.

"Look, Monica, is there any way we can sit and talk?"

His voice wavers, and the desperation in his eyes is almost laughable. Almost.

But I've got nothing to say to him.

I open my dry mouth to respond, but the sound that escapes isn't mine.

It's a scream.

"Everybody get the fuck down!"

I whip my head toward the entrance. Three masked men burst into the pub, guns waving wildly. My heart slams against my ribs as I spot them. Dad and Cathay—thank God—they'd gone to the stockroom just as Chase arrived.

The pub erupts into chaos. Patriots duck under tables, chairs scrape against the floor, glass smashes. Near the bar, a woman furtively dials 999. Her eyes meet mine, and she gives a slight nod. I return it, subtle but tense.

"Monica, stay behind me."

Chase steps in front of me, shielding me instinctively. I try to sink lower behind the bar, but I'm too slow.

"You!"

The tallest of the masked men points his gun at me. My body locks in place, a statue of fear.

"Empty the fucking cash register, or I'll shoot!"

Does this idiot not realise nobody carries cash anymore? The till probably has enough for a bus fare at best.

"Bitch, I said empty it!"

The click of the safety shatters my thoughts.

Oh God. Oh God.

"I'm counting to three."

Shit. Shit. Shit.

"One."

Do something.

"Two."

Do what, though?

"Three."

"NOOOOO!"

The bang is deafening.

I squeeze my eyes shut, collapsing to my knees behind the bar. My hands slap against the cold tiles, and my breathing shatters into panicked gasps.

I run my hands over my body, frantic, searching for any sign of blood. A shaky breath escapes when I come up empty.

"You fucking idiot! You weren't supposed to shoot anyone!" one of the masked men snarls.

The pub doors swing open and slam shut. They're gone. Thank God.

Muted murmurs ripple through the room as people begin to emerge from their hiding spots. My eyes scan the space, but something's wrong. Where's Chase?

Panic rises in my chest as I step out from behind the bar. It takes only a second to find him, crumpled on the floor where he'd been standing.

"Oh my God."

My hands fly to my mouth as I stare at the blood staining his white shirt, spreading, pooling around his shoulder. Someone shouts that an ambulance is on its way.

I drop to my knees beside him, trembling. My cardigan is off in an instant, balled up and pressed against the wound. Blood seeps through the fabric, warm and sticky against my hands.

"Chase, stay with me. Please."

His eyelids flutter as he looks up at me, his brown eyes dim but focused.

"Monica…"

"Shh." My voice cracks as I try to soothe him. "Don't talk. The ambulance is coming. Just hold on."

He grimaces, trying to form words.

"You're going to be okay, Chase," I whisper, stroking his soft hair as tears blur my vision.

A faint smile tugs at his lips.

"Marry me. Marry me, Monica."

A laugh slips out, bitter and choked. Now? He picks now?

"Chase, just stay still. Don't—"

"Please."

The desperation in his voice cuts deep, twisting the knife already lodged in my chest. He blinks up at me, his gaze pleading, as if this answer means more than his own survival.

My dad bursts out of the stockroom and drops to the floor beside us.

"Okay," I whisper, my voice barely audible over the chaos in my head. "Yes. I'll marry you."

Relief washes over his face, and his eyes drift closed, a small smile frozen in place.

"Chase?" My voice rises. "Chase, stay with me!"

Nothing.

"Fuck! Chase!"

Paramedics rush in, pushing me aside. I stumble back, helpless as they strap him to machines, attaching wires and tubes with practiced urgency. The sight of his still body on the gurney makes my stomach churn.

They lift him, rushing him out of the pub.

"Let's go," my dad says firmly, pulling me up. "We'll follow the ambulance in my car."

I nod numbly, letting him guide me to the car park. My legs move, but the rest of me feels frozen. My mind is a void, unable to think, unable to process.

I can't lose him. Not now.

35 CHASE

The last words I heard replay in my head, echoing exactly what I was for stepping into that pub: a fucking idiot.

It had been over a month since I last saw Monica, and I won't lie—I've been a wreck.

The office hadn't been the same since she quit. That Monday morning, I broke the news to the team, telling them she'd left the company for good. Questions flew at me, but I brushed them off, retreating into my office and locking the door for the rest of the day.

I eventually gave in and reached out to Jane to apologise for what happened.

I know I can be cold at times but Monica made me want to be a better person.

That meant apologising for my mistakes. Jane had emailed back saying thank you for my apology and also updated me on how she'd found a job located in London.

Everything about the office felt off. The space, once so alive, seemed muted and dull. At one point, I even called in electricians to check the lighting, convinced something must be wrong. They assured me everything was perfectly normal, but nothing about it felt normal.

Normal had been Monica. Normal was seeing her every morning at work and every evening after. It was her falling asleep against me and me waking her the next day with a gentle touch to her hair. Normal was the life we had before I let it fall apart.

I told myself—no, forced myself—not to reach out. I couldn't stomach the thought of hurting her any more than I already had. But in the end, I gave in.

She'd been graceful, of course. She mailed my belongings back to me, even though we lived only minutes apart. Polite. Detached. Meanwhile, I clung to her things, selfishly keeping them in the hope she'd come by to get them.

I wanted her to show up. I wanted a chance to say all the things I couldn't that day—the words that still sat heavy on my chest.

My eyes flutter open, greeted by a stark white ceiling. The steady beeping of a monitor beside me anchors me to reality. Slowly, I scan the room.

Carlos, Rain, Cathay, Jordan, Noah, and even Skye are gathered around my hospital bed, their faces lit with relieved smiles.

Cathay clutches Carlos's arm tightly, as if letting go might make the moment unreal. Jordan's arms are draped over Rain's shoulders, holding her close, while Noah gently strokes Skye's hand where it rests between them. Their collective relief is palpable.

But one face is missing.

Where's Monica?

My chest tightens as I struggle to recall what happened after the gunshot. My memories are a jumbled mess, the details slipping through my fingers like sand. I open my mouth to ask, but the door creaks open before I can speak.

She walks in, her eyes glassy, brimming with unshed tears. She whispers down the phone 'he's awake, I'll tell him to call you both later. Bye Sofia' before hanging up and walking over to me.

Relief floods through me, overwhelming and all-encompassing. She's here. She's safe.

Jordan clears his throat, breaking the moment. "We'll give you two some privacy," he says, guiding everyone out. One by one, they shuffle toward the door, leaving us alone.

"Hi," she says softly, stepping closer.

"Hi," I reply, my voice hoarse.

Her hand brushes my face, and I instinctively nuzzle into it, savouring her touch.

"I'm sorry," we both blurt out at the same time. A laugh bubbles up between us, lightening the heaviness in the air.

"How long was I out?" I ask, wincing as I shift to sit up.

Monica perches on the edge of the bed, just by my feet. "About a day," she explains gently. "They took you straight into surgery to remove the bullet. You've got yourself a nasty wound, Mr. Hero."

A smile tugs at my lips, though her words stir a memory—faint but undeniable. Oh God. I asked her to marry me, didn't I?

And… Did she say yes?

Everything she wrote in the letter she left on her desk the day she quit comes rushing back. The hurt I caused her. The trust I shattered. My fists clench as I remember the words—each one a punch to my gut. I've never been so disappointed in myself. She wrote that, in a way, she'd forgiven me, that it had made her stronger. But I can't forgive myself. Not now, not ever. I'll spend the rest of my life trying to make it right—if she'll let me.

Monica interrupts my spiralling thoughts, lifting her left hand with a grin so bright it could outshine the sun. "I guess we should make this official?"

My heart skips a beat. Oh, fuck. She said yes.

I try to lean toward her, but the sharp pain in my shoulder stops me short. She rises from her spot, moving closer, standing just within arm's reach.

"You mean it?" I ask, my voice barely above a whisper.

Her gaze softens, full of a love I don't deserve but desperately want. "I do, Chase."

I raise my good arm, cupping the back of her neck to pull her down. When our lips meet, it's like the world falls away, leaving only her.

In that moment, I vow to make her the happiest woman alive.

When we pull apart, her eyes remain glassy, though a wide smile curves her lips.

"We have things to work through," she says quietly, "but I want to be with you. Seeing you like that…" Her voice breaks, and she blinks back tears.

My throat tightens as my own eyes sting. "I never want to lose you either, Monica," I say, the words tumbling out with raw emotion. "I will spend the rest of my life making it up to you. Make me the happiest man alive and marry me?"

I ask her again, needing to hear the answer when I'm fully conscious this time.

"Yes, Mr. Marino," she says, her voice steady yet brimming with joy. "I'll marry you."

She leans in once more, pressing her lips to mine—this time as my fiancée.

EPILOGUE
MONICA

My engagement ring catches the glow of the Christmas tree lights, sparkling like the fresh snow falling outside in the quiet Verona evening. Chase's arms wrap snugly around my waist, his warmth pressing against my back. I lean my head against his shoulder, sighing contentedly.

"One year from today, mia cara, and you'll be Mrs Chase Marino," he murmurs, his voice low.

A smile tugs at my lips as I hum in response.

"That does sound pretty good, doesn't it?"

It's hard to believe how far we've come since that chaotic night.

The hospital discharged Chase a few days after his surgery, though he still grumbles about his weekly physio sessions at the local clinic.

I made a deal with him: every time he goes, I'll have his favourite dinner waiting for him when he gets home. The promise always coaxes a smile from him—though it never stops the complaining.

Not long after his release, I packed up my apartment and moved in with him. The same day, he made everything official, dropping to one knee to propose properly. I reached over to the final box that needed unpacking. Teasing me as we unpacked my things, constantly moving the box around, passing it to me and then taking it from my hands again. He eventually gave up playing his little game and let me open the box. Inside was a small velvet black box surrounded by a bulk of my favourite red lipstick.

My eyes immediately filled with tears.

After the trauma of almost loosing Chase, I never wanted to be without him again.

While I screamed "Yes!"—over and over, he lifted me off my feet and spun me around, grinning like a fool. That grin faded a little when he winced from the effort, earning him a whack from me to his good shoulder.

The aftermath of that night at the pub was a whirlwind. When the police arrived to investigate, we learned that Cathay's sons had orchestrated the robbery. They'd been trying to blackmail her for weeks, forcing her to empty the cash register during her shifts. She stood up to them, refusing to comply and they threw a tantrum—one that ended with Chase taking the brunt of their rage.

My dad chose to believe Cathay's side of the story, and their relationship survived the ordeal. A few weeks later, Cathay decided to sell her café. She told us it was once a source of pride, a way to support her children after their father passed, but now it held too many painful memories for her. With no intention of leaving anything to her sons, she cut ties completely.

My dad was over the moon when I told him the news of mine and Chase's engagement. Cathays eyes filled with tears as she brought me in for a hug.

I finally have a daughter.

She whispered against my ear that day. She knew about the history with my mum, but she didn't know what that meant to me when she said that sees me as her daughter.

Chase's mother calls from the kitchen, her cheerful voice carrying through the house.

"Dinner's ready."

He begins to turn to walk out of the room.

"Wait, I want to show you something".

He furrows his eyebrows at me.

I slowly lift my dress and turn to reveal a matching red lace bra and thong set with his name across the back.

A moan escapes his lips.

"Monica, are you trying to kill me?"

A soft giggle escapes my lips, the sound light and unrestrained. I adore this back-and-forth, the playful teasing that feels like our own private language. It's what I live for, what keeps my heart racing. It's why I fell so deeply, hopelessly in love with him. He straightens me up and crashes his lips onto mine.

How quickly can we eat dinner so we can go upstairs?

Chase takes my hand, tangling our fingers together as we make our way to the dining room. The aroma of Sofia's traditional Italian Christmas feast fills the air, rich and comforting. Jordan smirks at me as Chase pulls out my chair.

I glance to my left, catching my best friend mid-sip of wine, her cheeks already flushed. She's been talking to Jordan all evening with an intensity that hasn't escaped my notice.

Mental note: corner her about that later.

"Saluti!" The toast erupts around the table, everyone clinking glasses and laughing.

I lean back, letting the joy of the moment wash over me. This is everything I could have ever wanted. Chase and I have talked through so much, and in the new year, I'll be returning to Be Creative—not as his employee this time, but as his business partner.

It feels like all the pieces of my life are finally falling into place. Well… almost all of them.

A few weeks ago, I received an email from my mother. She wrote to inform me about a distant relative's passing, I offered her my condolences and in return she asked to meet. I'd barely finished reading it before I blocked her address.

I'd told my dad about the email, expecting him to react strongly, but all he said was, "It's your choice." One look at the expression on his face, and I knew I'd made the right decision. She doesn't deserve a place in my life anymore—not when I'm finally surrounded by people who truly love and support me.

"Amore mio?" Chase whispers, pulling me out of my thoughts.

I looked up at him, startled.

"Yes, Chase?"

"I love you."

I smile, my heart swelling with affection. "I love you too."

THE END

ACKNOWLEDGEMENTS

To my incredible ARC readers – your enthusiasm, feedback, and kind words have meant the world to me. Thank you for being part of this journey and helping bring this story to life.

To my amazing sister. You're the Rain to my Monica. Thank you for everything.

And to my husband – thank you for letting me pick your brain at all hours of the day. Your patience and encouragement are the glue that held this book (and me!) together.

This book wouldn't be here without all of you.

ABOUT THE AUTHOR

Hi readers.
Thank you so much for taking the time to read We've Met Before, the first book in the Serendipity series. It means the world to me to have your support on this journey!
. I am a self-published living in the Midlands, UK. I set WMB in Manchester because it's one of my favourite cities. When I'm not reading and writing, I work as a graphic designer and marketing executive and enjoy spending time with my husband, my friends and my family.

Please follow my socials to keep up with the latest updates.
@miriamoboyeauthor

Stay tuned for Rain and Jordan's story.

Printed in Dunstable, United Kingdom

65837120R00178